Valley of Fire

Valley of Fire

Janet Cox

Deseret Book Company
Salt Lake City, Utah

Library of Congress Cataloging in Publication Data

Cox, Janet, 1947—
  Valley of fire.

  I. Title.
PS3553.09194V3 1983   *813'.54*   *83-20966*
ISBN 0-87747-985-2

First printing November 1983

To Mom and Dad—Grant and Blanche Gibby—with love

ACKNOWLEDGMENTS

I wish to thank the many close friends, family members, and others who assisted in numerous ways in the preparation of this book. Those who helped significantly with historical information, research, personal interviews, suggestions, and encouragement are Misha Bigler, John Bromley, Elder Vaughn J. Featherstone, Ingelise Gibby, Andrew Karl Larson, Walter and Eva Miles, Amanda Milne, Frank Reed, Richard Russell, Carol Seegmiller, and Roger and Pam Stratford.

In a special way I would like to thank my sister, Susan Hancock, and her husband, Larry Hancock, for their generosity in opening their home to me during my weeks of research in St. George.

ONE

It was an ancient Concord—a "pitching Betsy," as truckers had called the lumbering coaches in the earliest days of the Wells Fargo Stage Lines. From the tattered appearance of the interior, it had been in use decades before—maybe even when the famous Butterfield name blazoned every stage running between St. Louis and Salt Lake City.

Why Melvin Stubbs had hired such an outlandish rig for us was beyond me, and I wanted to complain of it to his bride. But we'd reached the summit of another hard-won rise, and the view, falling away almost from under us, stole my breath. I clung to my seat and said another prayer that the driver, Willis, had stopped drinking and would keep us on the road.

The terrain was terrible, and it had been getting progressively worse since our departure from the train at Milford. That had been only yesterday, only two days, though they'd seemed like ten what with all the stops and starts, the dirt, the constant jostling, and now the growing intensity of the heat. *Heat!* I pressed a cloth to my damp throat. What it was going to be like down in the lower country I dreaded to imagine.

Debra sneezed and swiped at the eddies of dust between us. "Today's worse! If we don't make it by tonight, I don't know what I shall do. I can't take another day of this, and I've told Mel." She flurried a hand down the front of her blouse, which only served to manufacture more of the red clouds. "Oh, Delores," she wailed, "isn't it awful? I feel I've been kicked and kicked in the backside, and I'm fed up with inhaling this stupid dust. My eyes sting, my throat hurts—" She sniffed, and then giving way, blew her nose with complete, unladylike abandon.

I laughed. My younger sister was usually so prim and proper. "What a sight you are, Deb. If your Mary were along, she'd order Mel and Willis to pull up and douse you in a stream, head and all!"

She ignored me and scrubbed at her nose, though her efforts did as much damage as good. Her hanky was like mine—caked with the horrid powder, as was everything in sight. "Huh, you should talk, sister dear, your complexion, *your complexion*—" Despite herself she began to giggle. "—it matches your hair—flaming red. You could pass for one of those Indians at Juab, you could. You should see yourself!" The peals of laughter came again.

I smiled, glad that she had forgotten her miseries so easily and wished that, somehow, I could do the same.

The hills, craggy and towering, were widening out some and with them the road. Breathing easier, I caught a glimpse of a pass and through it the top of a crimson-rimmed valley. Was it St. George at last? My only other visit had been as a child years ago, but the memory of red, red, sun-scorched hills and ash-black cliffs was firm in my mind. It still seemed miles away and not the least inviting. If the waves of heat dancing like ghost flames in the arid nothingness were anything to judge it by, it was an orange hole burning in the desert—a valley of fire—and Papa, Papa was sending me down into it.

"Well, aren't you going to do anything about it at all?" Debra was asking.

2

"About what?"

"Your face. It's filthy."

"What's the use, and who is there to see me in this forsaken place?"

Debra scowled. "Oh, go on and cry! Why on earth don't you? Let it out before we arrive, and you'll feel better."

"And what is there to cry about?"

"Why can't you admit you're hurting? If I were you, Lori, I'd have been in tears the entire way. I mean it. And here we're nearly to Clara's and still you won't even talk about it. Why?"

"Would it change anything, Deb? I just need to give Papa some time, that's all. It shall all blow over in a few weeks' time, and then he'll want me home with him again. Egan may be his friend, but I'm his daughter. And when he learns that you won't be going back, he'll be all the more anxious to make amends with *me*."

"You really don't see it, do you? Papa said as much to me. He said, 'Delores doesn't understand why I'm sending her off to Clarey's. But until she does, and until she makes drastic changes in her shameful behavior, I won't have her back.'"

I felt a stab of pain. "Papa said that to you?"

Debra settled back against the sweat-stained cushions. "He did. We had a long, long talk about it. He has to talk to *someone!* Delores, you've gotten yourself into a frightful fix, and the sooner you admit it, the sooner you can right things. Papa has been humiliated. He isn't going to forget and forgive as easily as you think. Grandmother's not there now to soothe his anger. He's kicked you out. You're twenty-two and without prospects. How you must feel! Here you've been the favored one for so long—Grandmother Rachael's own darling, and only six months after her death, Papa gives you the heave-ho. I'd be stricken."

"Well, I'm not stricken—not in the least." The lie came easily to my lips, and the vague smile faded from Debra's face. "Would you like it better if I were?"

3

"I'd understand, that's all. You really are a most difficult person to know, Delores. Nothing gets at you. Mary says—"

"Mary says far too much for a servant—takes too much on herself; and so do you! What? Would you have me marry that old . . . old . . ." I struggled to find a label that wouldn't be too condemning. After all, I had worn Egan Stone's ring for nearly a year. ". . . eccentric just to save face? Some loyalty you have, Debra Ashley!"

"Debra *Stubbs*, remember? And *I* never asked you to go get engaged, but once you did and flaunted it like that— riding in his elegant carriage with your nose in the air, well, you should have had the common decency to go through with it. How could you change your mind just days before the wedding—how could you?"

"Debra, don't—"

"You used him, Delores, and you used Papa, too. And why? Egan was everything you say you want—wealthy, well-positioned, and his children—"

"Oh, by all means don't forget them!"

"The little one loved you. Haven't you any heart?"

I didn't even flinch. "None." I met Debra's stare. "Now, can we drop it?"

"Do you know I *almost* believe that." Debra went on as if she hadn't heard my flat request. "You know, not counting Grandmother's funeral, I've only once seen you cry, really cry. Want to know when that was?"

"Debra—"

"It was when your Mark up and married Anna Carrow! How you carried on."

"Oh, you really are such a goose, Debra. I hardly re-4   member the man."

"It hasn't been that long since he left you high and dry."

"Drop it, Debra Sue or I'll start in on you and Mel!" The threat had the desired effect, for Debra was silent a moment, and then lifted her head indignantly.

"What could you possibly say about Mel and me? I'm happy we've gone ahead and married. I have no regrets. He could have had anyone, you know."

I thought of the lank, wiry-haired blond who was now my sister's husband. He was rugged and attractive, but then Debra was so easily pleased. She was going to be dirt poor her entire life. It still seemed strange that Debra would have the nerve to up and marry on the journey down here. What with the traveling accommodations and everything, they hadn't had a minute's time alone together. "Debra, you aren't telling me something. I can feel it. And why didn't you insist that Mel take you to the temple?"

"Shhh. What if he hears?" She pulled a face, gesturing to the open window. Mel had long since been driven out of the stagecoach by the airless heat, and was riding on top with the driver.

"He hasn't earned the right to go to the temple, has he! I'm glad you won't be there when Papa learns you've married beneath yourself. *You* could have had anyone, Debra. You're lovely and you're an Ashley. You could have had station and wealth! Why you ever picked a farmer, and one from such a simple family—"

"Don't you dare talk against Mel. Don't you dare, or I'll desert you in St. George."

"Oh, Debra, don't go overreacting. I'm merely trying to be loyal to you."

"You can be loyal by accepting the fact that I've married the most wonderful man ever. I know that it seems impossible to fall in love so quickly, but I have. Besides, I've done it and I can't be looking back."

"So—" I strained against the jostling and rubbed at the ache in my back, "you are having regrets!"

"No, I'm not. It's just that I wish I could have told Papa . . ." Her shoulders lifted, and she began to cry.

The sun was in the west now, and the air would soon be cooling. We'd be able to breathe again. I closed my eyes

5

against the dreary picture outside the coach, and telling myself we were nearly there, I tried to sleep, but Debra's little crying noises made it impossible.

"Oh, Debra!" I rubbed an impatient hand over my eyes. "Stop sniveling! As you said, you're married and can't go looking back."

"You're jealous, Delores. Oh, yes you are! You can pretend all you like, but you feel horrid to be the only daughter left unmarried—'specially when you're so much *older* than I am. So what if you're smarter and prettier, you're bossy. Bossy and colder than an iceberg, and what man wants that?"

A headache had begun throbbing behind my temples, and I yearned to be out of the smelly coach. "Debra, I'm tired. Let's just not talk anymore."

"Oh, now you're tired! After you've tried to poke holes in my happiness, *you* don't want to talk."

"To tell you the truth, I'm not feeling at all well. I know I've made you angry, but I haven't the strength anymore to follow the conversation."

Her eyes swept over me in a quick unsympathetic assessment.

"Besides, we need each other. We shouldn't be fighting. It's the infernal heat, don't you think? It's got us both on edge. Let's think of pleasant things—like a huge sparkling tub of water and Clara's scrumptious cooking and days and days of sleep. Doesn't that sound good?"

She nodded, but there was a curious flicker in her eyes. *Bridal nerves,* I thought. Tonight she wouldn't be able to postpone really becoming a wife, and that had to be terrifying. I remembered only too well the sick panic I felt every time Egan got that sensual gleam in his eyes.

"Will you two be staying at Cottonstreet, or will you be going on home to wherever it is that Mel lives?"

"Mel says we'll probably stay at the inn, and then tomorrow he'll drive me out to meet his mother and sister."

"Are you scared? I mean about tonight?" I knew she didn't like my asking, but I couldn't help myself.

It seemed impossible that my baby sister was married. She'd always been so protected by Papa and our governess, Mary Simms. While I'd been allowed to travel for my education, Debra had been kept safely at home in Ashley. It probably was no coincidence that her first time out from under Papa's eye, she'd done something rash.

"Scared?" She lay back against the corner of the coach. "Now who's being a goose? I've been married three days, and Mel's hardly had the chance to kiss me. It will be *heaven* being alone—becoming a wife." She studied the hands in her lap. "Being in love, I mean really, unselfishly in love, like *I* am, Delores, makes a big difference, and since you haven't felt that way, you wouldn't understand."

"No, I suppose I wouldn't." I closed my eyes and willed the sleep to come.

* * * * *

There was a shout, a mingling of men's voices and laughter, and I opened my eyes to darkness. The coach had stopped. Had we arrived or only paused again to water the horses? Torches burned outside, and beyond the glare, I strained to see the outline of buildings, but saw only blackness.

"Sit back," Debra hissed, "and let Mel and Willis handle it!"

"Handle what?" My sleep-glazed eyes cleared, and I saw a half circle of mounted riders, carrying torches, close in about the stagecoach. They weren't masked, and by the banter outside, the group was obviously friendly.

"Just keep still, Delores, and everything will be all right."

I smiled at my sister's dramatics. "Of course everything will be all right. Willis and Mel know these men."

"Yes, I know, but—" She stopped, and I felt her staring

7

at me through the darkness. "Wouldn't you like to wash up quickly?" A cool, damp cloth was pressed against my cheek. "Delores, I'm sorry, but I do owe first allegiance to Mel, and he made me promise not to tell you. We hoped to avoid all this by taking a longer route, but then Willis refused to do that, and—"

"Tell me what?" I took the cloth from her to finish the job. "Oh, Debra, what are you talking about?"

"That looks better." She ignored my question. "But there is still a smudge on your chin, and your hair is falling out in back."

"Debra, tell me!" But there was no chance for her to answer, for the door was suddenly jerked open, a torch was thrust up to the window, and an unshaven face leered at us. His eyes gleamed yellow in the light, and his mouth parted to reveal uneven, broken teeth. "They're beauties, both of 'em. Raleigh was right about that, but which is which?" A hand reached for me, and I ducked, calling with a cool voice to the men above.

"Mel, Mel? Willis? What *is* all this?"

The coach creaked as someone jumped down to the ground. "Come on, Chaunce, you're frightening the girls. Step aside, and I'll help them out." It was Mel.

"Don't try nothin' tricky," Chaunce warned with another leer at me. "You're sly, pal, but remember your own rule. It goes easier for the bride if the groom cooperates!"

"Yes, and remember this, old man." Mel's tone sounded almost jovial, but held an underlying thread of menace. "If anyone hurt my girl—even accidentally—I'd take his head off, and you know I can do it." Silence fell on the group like a weight, and I sidled a little closer to the far side. Mel laughed then, and I breathed easier at his show of confidence. "What do you say you all escort us in, and we can continue this little gathering at Clarey's?"

"You'd like that, wouldn't you?" one of the men shouted. "But you set the rules a long time ago, Mel Stubbs.

You've made your bed, and you're going to have to lie in it alone tonight!"

Rowdy laughter and crudities rang from all sides, and I guessed there must be two dozen men out there. Poor Debra. I now understood her earlier fear. These men wanted to abduct her—separate her from her husband on their wedding night. Papa heartily disapproved of such goings on, and nothing like it had ever happened to any of my sisters, but then, they had married refined men. These nightmarish pranks were not allowed in their social circles. Debra must be regretting her hasty marriage all the more with this to face.

"Aw, just get them out, and let's have a look."

"Yeah, quit stalling, Mel!" Someone called out a threat, and Debra gasped.

"Easy guys, and watch your language, or you'll answer to me. These two are *ladies*." Mel leaned into the coach. "Come on, honey, Delores. You needn't worry, either of you. The guys sound worse than they are. They don't mean any harm." Mel lifted us out onto the ground and stood protectively between us with a comforting arm at my back. "Boys, meet my bride-to-be, Debra Ashley, and her older sister, Delores. I don't know where you got your information, but this here party is too blamed early. Debra and I will be getting hitched in two weeks' time, and you're all invited to the wedding."

"Mel, you must think we're stupid." A rider nudged his horse forward. "We ain't made any mistakes."

"Yeah, old boy, considerin' all the weddin' parties *you've* thrown!"

Mel surveyed the gathered group with complete calm. "You're on your toes, boys, I admit. But it's no good stealing the bride before she is one. Your information's off a wide mile. I'm not married yet. Tell them, Willis!"

The burly stagecoach driver replied noncommittally, "I ain't seen no ceremony, boys."

"Stubbs, one of your most recent victims, Raleigh Morris, telegrammed us, and he says you married in Juab to avoid this little honor. He says his source is reliable."

"Then he's pulled one on you, hasn't he?" Mel tossed back his head and laughed, hugging me to him.

It almost worked. A murmur rippled among the men, and then Chaunce jabbed an elbow in my side. "Your old man's slippery as they come, ma'am. But if he's speakin' truth and we're too early, we'll just throw you another party in two weeks. Old Mel deserves the extra attention!"

There was a roar of assent, and Chaunce's hand touched mine.

"Stop it!" I shrank from the contact with the repulsive stranger, and Mel's arm closed about my shoulder. "And I am *not*—"

"Take it easy, honey. Chaunce looks mean, but he's all right. Been drinking some, that's all."

Honey, Mel had called me. I flicked an alarmed glance toward Debra, but she was no longer on the other side of Mel. She'd stepped back into the shadows near the coach, her back pressing into the door, her dark head down.

"Come on, little lady. Debra, is it?" Chaunce's fingers closed on my elbow, and he jerked me easily from Mel's embrace. "Like Mel says, we're just friends a' his, and we're harmless as babes."

"But I'm not Debra! I'm not! Do something, Mel!" Mel allowed another man to take his place at my shoulder, and they pushed me roughly toward a waiting horse. It couldn't be happening. "Don't touch me, any of you. Don't you dare!" I fought them with all my might, buckling my knees and kicking their shins, but all attempts were in vain. I couldn't get free of them. There were suddenly too many, and my pleas for freedom seemed only to incite them further.

"Hey, settle down, Debra." Mel's voice cut through my cold panic, but his words were far from reassuring, his tone falsely affectionate. "They won't hurt you. They're all friends. I'm sorry, but they've found us out. And anyway, this sort of thing is done all the time down here. You just go ahead, and they'll deliver you safe and sound to Cottonstreet at dawn, won't you? Ernie? Chaunce? Connan?"

"But I'm not his wife! You've got us mixed up. I'm Delores Lyn; Debra's my sister!" I wanted to scream. How could he do it? It was incredible, but I could see now that Melvin Stubbs and my sister had known all along that this was going to happen, and they had planned it this way. If the men didn't fall for Mel's bluff about not being married, then they would pretend that I was his wife. Either way they were assured of remaining together. There was no way out of this. Fear froze further protests, and I could only stammer, "Tell them—*tell them*—"

"Hey, that's right, guys. You've got the sisters mixed up. The taller one is the younger one. That's Debra over there."

A raucous chorus of laughter drowned out his further pretended protests, and though I resisted with flying fists and threats, I was hoisted onto a horse and herded off into the night. Just before I lost sight of the coach, I saw Debra moving to Mel's side. His arm came around her, and the two shadows blended into one.

Riders pressed all about me, their grinning faces contorted and shadowy in the flicker of the torches. Their language was crude and foreign to my ears, and foul smells of sweat, alcohol, and tobacco blended nauseatingly. I tried to shut out the terrors that were suddenly rampant in my imagination. They wouldn't hurt me—they wouldn't. But just the same, I hugged my saddle horn and began to pray.

11

TWO

The night had grown blacker than ever, or maybe it only seemed so because I was close to the brilliance of the fire, and beyond the puny glow was wilderness. I held my back ramrod straight and hugged my arms about my middle to keep my shivering from being noticeable. I tried not to think of the men—strangers—lazying about on every side, talking, joking, laughing—drinking too, for occasionally I saw a bottle being passed about. Much of the language appalled me, and my one consolation was that I'd seen a woman here. Though she hadn't spoken to me, just the knowledge that at least one other female was in the camp was a comfort. She was a large woman and frumpily dressed—one of the wives, no doubt. But she seemed respectable enough—at least I wanted to believe she was.

"Why don't you eat something?" One of the men held a tin plate down to me. "You're hungry."

I ignored him and the offered food and continued to watch the flames. He waited a minute, standing over me with the plate in his outstretched hand. "Come on, now—" his voice lowered to a whisper, and he squatted down and pushed the tray firmly into my hands. "These men aren't your enemies, *Delores*."

12

"You know!" I started, but he put out a hand to quiet me.

"Let them think you're your sister—just eat." The light of the fire fell on his angular face, but the blunt features remained shadowy and were darker than those of his rowdy friends. Only his eyes seemed bright. His hair, straight and midnight black, was too long at his neck. He had an alien look about him, dangerous and dark, and a curious way of speaking. I shifted away.

"You needn't be afraid of me. I'm Jonas Luker, a friend of Mel's."

"Oh? Is that supposed to be a recommendation?" I couldn't prevent the sarcastic curl to my lip, for tears were hovering just behind my eyes. I was determined that no one would know how terrified I really was. "Your Mel Stubbs is a low, untrustworthy, unscrupulous creature. How my sister ever managed to find such a—a criminal attractive I shall never know!"

The man at my side knocked back his hat and laughed in a low, rolling sound that wasn't unpleasant. "So you've found poor Mel out for what he is, have you?"

"Are you any better? Or your friends here? This is abduction. None of you shall find it at all amusing when I file suit with the authorities."

"Miss Ashley, your anger only sweetens the game, don't you see that?" He smiled across the darkness. "Be smart and go along with the mix-up. Some here won't take it kindly that old Mel has had the best of them again. They'll be mad as blazes, and who'll they take their frustration out on? You!"

"I'll not go along with anything. I owe no allegiance to Mr. Stubbs. I demand to be taken to the inn on Cottonstreet and now. I'm warning you—the Ashleys have influence, and unless—"

"Eat." He shook his head. "Just eat!"

"Eat what?" I glared at the nondescript lumps of food

on the tin plate. "The smell is abominable, and I doubt if the plate is even clean. Take me to cousin Clara's or—"

"I know, you'll land the lot of us in jail. I hate to disillusion you, girl, but Sheriff Jem Kippen won't lift a hand to help you. He'll make a nice speech about local traditions and bid you good day. It's a game—nothing more."

"But it's not, it's not. I've been traveling for days. I'm tired, exhausted, and hungry, and *I've been abducted!*" My voice had been getting progressively louder when a rough hand brushed over my lips.

"*I've told you to hush!* You don't want to draw any more attention to yourself than necessary."

"How dare you touch me!"

"Better keep your distance, Jonas." Someone laughed from the far side of the campfire. "From the look of things, she's ready to throw them beans back in your face."

I lifted the plate, and the group became instantly watchful.

"Hey, hey," someone snickered, "looks like Mel's got himself a high-spirited little wife. Go on, ma'am, and give Jonas whatfor."

"Yeah, toss it, Mrs. Stubbs. Don't let Luker bully you."

My eyes ricocheted from the food to Luker's narrowed eyes, but before I'd considered further, he muttered something and knocked the thing clear. As the plate went flying into the brush, shouts and cheers sounded all around.

"Real pity she's taken." A gravelly voice moved up on my left. "Mel sure got hisself a pretty 'un." The ground crunched beneath his boots as he moved between Luker and myself. He was big—as tall as Jonas Luker, but even more unkempt and wild-looking, with pale straggling hair and a barbed, unshaven face.

14

"So tell us about you and Mel, Mrs. Stubbs." He bent and pulled me to my feet as chills of revulsion shot through me.

"I—there's nothing to tell."

"There's gotta be." His eyes traveled suggestively down the length of me. I took a backward step and searched the shadows for the woman, but she was nowhere to be seen. The mood of the men was altering, and I was afraid.

I tried taking the offensive. "What is your name?"

He smiled at that and, with an amused glance at his friends, drawled, "Connan Trouseman, ma'am."

"Take your hand off me, Connan Trouseman." I stared at the fingers gripping my wrist. It was a wintry gesture Grandmother Rachael had taught me as "just enough show of hauteur to keep a man at his distance."

Trouseman's pale eyes reflected a flash of doubt. His hand was falling away when someone shouted, "Ain't she something! She's got even Con worried, she has." The jibe goaded, and he grabbed me hard by the shoulders.

"Light one of them torches, Chaunce, and bring 'er here. We'd all like a closer look at the face that snagged Mel in such short order."

Whistles and a general commotion followed, and I felt a sick, sinking sensation that robbed me of all thought but escape. "Leave me alone." My plea wasn't even audible in the confusion. They weren't listening nor did they care.

"Turn around here, Debra, and let's have a look-see." A torch was thrust so close to me that the heat singed my hair, and I screamed and lunged backward. But the cook fire was behind me, and my movement caught a portion of my skirt afire. Hot flames billowed up my side. I turned to run from the fire, but was knocked sideways into the dust as a dozen hands beat at the skirt until it was nothing but a smoking ruin.

"You all right?" The stocky torchbearer spoke with concern. "Con can be stupid, but he didn't mean to hurt you, ma'am."

"Well, if she wouldn'ta jerked back like that—"

"That's truth!" The gravelly voiced ruffian spoke up for himself. "I's gentle with women, Mrs. Stubbs. It was pure

15

accident, and yer husband ain't got no call for a grudge with me."

I pushed up to my knees, blinked the dirt and smoke from my eyes, and began wiping the soot and weeds from my mouth. I was unhurt, except for my dress. It'd been only a traveling dress—one of four that meant absolutely nothing to me, but the sight of the gray yardage blackened and scorched, hanging in shards atop my equally spoiled petticoat, was the final straw. My eyes filled with tears, and one by one they rolled in a dirty track down my face.

"I'll make it right about the dress, honest to—" The blasphemy fell off his lips with sickening ease, and he offered me a hand. "Let me help you up, ma'am."

I flinched away in real fear.

"Aw, come on, yer jus' tired out. Lyle's wife's brought out a nice wagon for ya to sleep in, and—"

"The lady's had enough of you, Con. I'll show her to the wagon." It was Jonas, and for some reason I actually sobbed at the sound of his voice. I gripped the hand that reached down to me. The arm around my waist as he set me on my feet was solid and comforting. I'd forgotten my earlier distrust, for, out of all this bedlam, only he had his senses about him, and Mel's friend or no, I was grateful he was there.

"Take a walk, Luker—" The brutish Trouseman blocked the way. "You're not part of this anyways, so stop trying to take over."

"Enough is enough, Con. You're drunk through. Since I'm here, I'll watch after Mel's interests, and unless you want trouble now, and more from the groom, you'll keep your distance. Now, turn in." Jonas Luker led me away 16 from the fire. A general taunting chorus wished me *good night*.

"The worst of it appears to be over. You're lucky. These things have gotten way out of hand before."

"Lucky!" I choked with indignation. "After all that has happened, you can say that?"

"The men kept their distance, didn't they? And they treated you well enough, and that speaks of their high respect for Mel. They didn't do their usual round of kissing the bride, for instance. Even I was looking forward to that." There was laughter in his voice, and I bristled, my eyes shooting up to his dark profile.

"None of this is funny, Mr. Luker—not remotely!"

"I can't agree, Lady Delores. You ought to see that face of yours. I haven't seen dirtier on a woman. Hmmm . . ." I felt his eyes studying me. "Maybe that's why they let all the kissing pass."

"For whatever reason, I'm grateful. I'll try to remember to keep my face as smudged as possible until I get safely to Clara's." I hadn't meant to sound so waspish, but I was shaken and afraid, and the poise that carried me through the most trying circumstances had long since shattered.

"You do that, Lady Delores." His tone wasn't kind, and I felt my former dislike returning full force.

"The name, Mr. Luker, is Delores Lyn Ashley. You may call me *Miss Ashley*."

He laughed outright then, and his lips bent to my ear. "For now—just to keep the lid on things—why don't we settle on Mrs. Stubbs? Debra Stubbs, Melvin's anxious little bride—"

He was becoming offensive, and I stepped away. "Are you going to show me where I sleep?"

"You see the lantern through the brush there? That's the wagon, and you'll find Lyle Sackett's wife waiting. Thelma, though incredibly small-minded, is a good woman. She'll give you bedding and a piece of the wagon bed to sleep in. You'll be safe and comfortable enough, I'm sure. If you'd let yourself relax, you might discover how very pleasant sleeping under the stars can be."

I slapped at a hovering mosquito. "I'm sure I won't sleep a wink. Good night."

"I'd try hard to sleep if I were you." His voice followed me. "From what your cousin Charity tells me, you'll have

17

little rest from now on. Clara's of Cottonstreet is a might busy inn—renowned in these parts, and Clarey's ill—right off her feet, in fact. That will leave a lot in your hands. You were sent down here to work, weren't you?"

I stopped midway to the wagon. "Clarey's ill? Charity told you that?"

There was a gleam of teeth in the night. "Charity didn't have to *tell* me, Lady D. But then you'll find out all about it in the morning. Good night." He left me staring after him as he turned back toward the fire.

THREE

"Sit still! Can't you hang on better than that?" Jonas Luker railed over his shoulder as we climbed what he'd promised was the last ridge before our final descent into the valley. "A horse isn't a carriage, Lady Delores."

"I've told you not to call me that. I don't like it!"

"What are you doing? Just perching and hoping for the best? You're likely to take a bad fall and crack your pretty skull."

I wanted to tell him that I was really a fine horsewoman and that I had good reason for slipping all over the place. But the matter was too delicate to take up with a man. I'd bruised myself, and it was impossible to find a comfortable seat on the animal. Besides that, I was uneasy with my arms looped about a man's middle, a stranger's at that. *He* had no qualms though. Whenever I let my hold slacken the tiniest bit his hands were there to jerk mine back into place.

"This is the summit. We should be to Cottonstreet by ten anyway. Look! You can see part of the valley from here between those two ridges there."

I lifted my chin, but there was no use trying. I couldn't see much over the high shoulder and grimy shirt, but on our descent I spied the ridges, both a stark black, the one on

19

the east, less prominent than the other that hemmed in the western end of the basin. In the south a wide river meandered and blue mountains faded into the distance. I did like the river and the mountains. They softened the harsh ruggedness of everything else.

"Nice, huh?"

"Wild-looking."

"That's what makes it *nice*, Lady."

We rounded another hill, and the valley at last burst into full view. It was so good to finally see the place, see the end of my travels—St. George, with real buildings, businesses, homes and people—that I sighed relief.

"It is a sight for sore eyes." He halted the horse. "Like coming upon a green oasis in the desert."

It was greener, at least the city was, than I'd remembered, and the spires of the temple whiter. They glistened reassuringly in the morning light like new snow. The temple faced east, and the little city was north of it, the streets laid out in traditional Mormon order, wide and flanked with spacious lots around each home, allowing room in the center of each block for barns and corrals. Here, as in Ashley, most folks kept their own animals to sustain them—cows, horses, pigs, and chickens.

"And Clarey's place? Can you see that from here?"

"Too many trees."

* * * * *

Down in the city it was warm as we plodded along the dusty streets. I couldn't keep my eyes from the grass-banked ditches. They were brimming with water and made me thirst miserably for a drink. Two pesky flies droned about my head no matter how I swatted, and I pushed at the misarranged pins in my hair, trying not to feel self-conscious at the stares of those we passed.

"Aren't we about there?"

"Soon . . ."

20

Not soon enough. I swallowed, smiled at a little girl jumping rope in the dirt, her braids flying ribbons, and glanced north to the shock-red bluffs rising abruptly against the blue. Strange place . . . wild and strange. My heart began to slam inside my breast, and I closed my eyes. I would do well here. I would make myself like it no matter what, and with heaven's help Papa would forgive me and let me come home to him, and I would never, ever be so stupid again.

"You saying a prayer or something—"

The horse had stopped. I opened my eyes to Jonas's puzzled look. "Are we here?"

"Yup. There she is—Clara's of Cottonstreet."

The inn was smaller than I remembered it. Oh, it was good-sized for a house—about half as large as my family home in Ashley. But for such uncivilized country the peach stucco two-story was impressive and well-built, with a white balcony running the length of the upstairs rooms and turning about one side and with a long, white-railed porch beneath. It was well kept and clean-looking and boasted three mulberry trees in front. There was even grass beneath— patchy grass that grew, by the look of things, only where water and shade were most available, and both had to be rare commodities here, for it was *hot!*

I allowed Jonas Luker to hand me down off the horse before he dismounted, and I nearly ran through the green picket gate up the worn path and onto the wooden porch steps. *I was here and nothing too terrible had happened after all.* My eyes pricked with emotion, and I paused before opening the door to gather my composure.

"Wait, and I'll go in with you." Jonas tied the horse and ambled up the path. "Just to reassure Charity and Clarey that even with the tattered dress and tousled hair their 'Ashley cousin' is in one piece."

"You needn't, Mr. Luker." I avoided his eyes. The man had assumed the position of my protector, and while I may have needed it at the camp, this was an entirely different matter. He was good looking in a dark-skinned way and was probably used to the attentions of women. It wouldn't do at all to allow him to continue the familiar manner he'd adopted with me. I knew nothing about him except what Thelma Sackett had confided—that he was the son of a half-breed Paiute woman, and too, that he was "inappropriately friendly" with Charity Raines—Clarey's married daughter.

"Best watch yourself with that one, Mrs. Stubbs," Thelma's parting words warned. "Beneath that civilized exterior he's got that wild blood."

"I can tell cousin Clara myself." I waved him away. "Your . . . your assistance has been appreciated. You may go now." My words were more of a dismissal than thanks, and Jonas Luker received them with a tightening jaw.

"Lady Delores, I'm coming in with or without your permission. This is more my home than yours, and I can tell you that Charity will be much happier to see me than you."

There it was! I watched his approach with widening eyes. He'd as much as admitted his attachment for Charity. So what Thelma Sackett had said was true. "You *live* here?"

"For the time being, yes, I do." The news depressed me, though I tried not to show it, and without further discussion I opened the door and stepped inside the rather austere entry. It was flanked on one side by a large parlor and on the other by a dining room. Both were empty, and I proceeded to the back of the inn where I knew the kitchen was.

"Clara? Charity?"

"I'm coming! I'm coming!" A door closed, and I looked down the hall to see Clara's daughter hurrying toward me with an expression that left me uncertain about my welcome.

I remembered that my other visit here eight years ago had left me baffled as to how Charity felt about me. Of course, she'd been eighteen then and up-in-the-air in love with the flamboyant Randall Raines, and I suppose she could be forgiven for not taking much notice of a young second cousin. Raines had been handsome enough to divert any girl's attention—a suave, swaggering fellow with too much popularity and charm. The family had been delighted with Charity's choice of a husband. Not now. It had proved a troubled marriage from the beginning and had brought Charity nothing but humiliation, heartache, and two rather "wild" children—at least that was Papa's point of view. It was no secret that Randall Raines was in prison for embezzlement, leaving his wife to care for her small family herself. She'd moved back to Cottonstreet to help her mother run the inn. But Charity had weathered the years well. She was older, but maturity had only heightened her loveliness, and her face, except for a vertical crease running now between her eyes as she studied me, was as unblemished as ever.

"Hello, Charity. I must look quite horrible, I know." I held out a steady hand.

She gave me a tired, unfriendly nod, and I felt a creeping intimidation. "That will be the day, cousin. Welcome." She touched my hand with her own. "I'm relieved to see you've survived Mel's rowdy bunch."

"Yes, so am I. I was quite terrified at first. If my sister or Mel had thought to warn me . . ."

She nodded with the same exasperation I was feeling. "They did play quite an awful trick on you, didn't they?" She lifted gray eyes to Jonas Luker waiting in the entry behind me. "We have Jonas to thank, you know, for riding along." She gave him then what she'd withheld from me—a real smile that softened her features and magically lit her pale eyes. "You don't know how it eased Mama's mind, Jonas, to know you'd be there. Thank you so much for coming to the rescue."

I turned to see his answering nod. "My pleasure, Charity. My pleasure." He angled a grin then at me as if to point out that I hadn't thanked him at all. "Now tell us about Clarey. Is she doing any better? Did Hallum make it by again?"

"Oh, quite late, but he says there's really nothing to be done but to make Mama stay down this time and to keep her from fretting. It's worry, he says, that aggravates her leg, and I'll tell you, all this commotion over Delores and—" Her tone switched to one of faint accusation as she broke off with a sigh. "Oh, I'm not blaming you, Delores. It's just that it's been such a night." She looked to Jonas for sympathy. "Wubbles was up complaining about his kettle of ailments, and the children have misbehaved at every turn. To top it all off, Miles Lassiter is due back *tomorrow* and his room is literally torn apart. I haven't had a minute to see to that. I don't know how I shall get it all done."

"Take heart, Char." Jonas winked. "You've got me, and now you've got Miss Ashley here to help out. What can we do?"

"Well, for starters, you could check on the children. They're out back, and then bring in some water, will you? Delores could begin with the breakfast dishes—they're piled high, I'm afraid. And the upstairs cleaning isn't half done. Meg's girls have gone to fetch something for Wubbles."

"Cleaning?" I looked from one to the other and half laughed. "Cousin Clara said in her letter that I would be more of a *hostess*—entertaining at the piano, singing, and conversing with guests. Of course I shall be happy to do those things that I've been trained in and such—"

"And such?" Charity seemed prepared to do battle. I smiled at her rising color and tried to keep my tone casual and offhand.

"Yes, I do needlework of all kinds, and I've been trained in every area of the cultural arts. If you have a spare room, I could begin a school that—"

"For now, Delores, we need your help in other areas,

and I'm afraid 'cleaning up' heads the list. Mama will be off her feet for weeks, and while I'd love to have you sing for your supper, that doesn't quite cover your keep, especially when there're only me, Meg Gibbons, and her girls to do the work here. At the moment only half the rooms are in use, but on the weekends we always have a full house. We shall all have to keep hopping to even keep up."

"But I've never done cleaning in my life."

"That's quite a confession, but you shall learn."

"Charity," I sputtered, dismayed at her attitude, "you ought to employ my help where I'll do you the most good. I know Clara is ill, but I won't hesitate to go to her and demand that she keep her original agreement."

"You shall do no such thing." Charity's eyes seemed to take fire, and she took a menacing step toward me. "I'm sorry I cannot enlist your aid voluntarily, Delores Lyn, but you have been quite thrust upon us. I have your father's letter here." She snatched the pale, green paper from her pocket and waved it at me. "By your own careless behavior, you are in disgrace and have been sent to work here as we see fit. We didn't ask for this responsibility, and as Mama is out of the picture right now, I must make the decisions. You will not upset her by whining about your duties, or I shall put you on the next stage north."

"Charity, you needn't make threats. I'm sure we can work out this difference of opinion civilly. I shall be quite happy to do my part—"

"Good, I'm happy to hear it. Let's get you settled, and then you can begin. Debra and Mel left your trunks here last night—all *four* of them," she emphasized with disgust, "and they're in your room upstairs. Jonas, she's in number 7. Will you show her where that is? Oh, and you'll find the tubs in the small room just off the kitchen. There are clean towels there too, but please don't be extravagant with them. Is there anything else you need?"

I could only stare at her dumbfounded. Never in my entire life had I been so ill treated. And her jibe about being extravagant with the towels was the last straw. Obviously she very much resented my privileged upbringing.

"I could stand some courtesy," I finally said. "It's true I have been *thrust* upon you, as you put it, but neither did *I* ask for the honor. It's been a trying night for me too, and an exhaustingly long and dirty trip. I shall take my bath, and I shall also take some necessary sleep as I've had practically none for a week. After that, I will be down to resume my duties, whatever they may be. It will be much pleasanter for both of us if you drop the whip. I'm not in the least intimidated by your bullying, Charity."

I turned toward the front of the house and went up the stairway. Jonas Luker hadn't said a word. It was obvious I was without allies here, and that was just fine with me.

The room was another disappointment. It was a tiny box with one curtained window. A narrow bed with a faded patchwork quilt was its only adornment. A ridiculously old-fashioned washstand and bowl and a kerosene lantern stood on a squat table by the bed. It was a far cry from my own room at Ashley Heights. I hated to spend even one night in such dreary quarters. I'd write Papa immediately—no, I'd telegram—and say whatever was needed to get back into his good graces. The thought of leaving did help a little.

Anticipating my early departure from the miserable circumstances in which I had found myself, I unpacked only a few of my things, bathed—using only two towels—returned to my room, and fell instantly asleep.

The sun was in the west when I opened my eyes. Except for feeling stiff and some rather sharp hunger pains, I felt

26 better. I rummaged through my clothes and donned a lightweight, green silk dress and tied a spotless white apron over it. My aprons had been made to order with snugly fitting bodices and scalloped skirts. I had six of them, each trimmed in crisp eyelet or gathered lace. They were more of a decoration than anything, but they made me look more

like a professional hostess. I swept up my hair with pearled combs, brushed some color on my lips and cheeks, and descended the stairs, ready for whatever was to come.

Jonas Luker paused below me on the stairs. He too had cleaned up and was wearing a leather vest atop a blue shirt—the same shade as his eyes—and brown pants that hugged his long legs. As I met his gaze, I couldn't help thinking how ruggedly attractive he was—not that I personally could ever be interested in such a man, but still, he was admittedly nice to look at.

I ignored the jerk in my pulses as he watched me come toward him. He said nothing for a moment, but his blue eyes took in every detail of my appearance, and I was glad at the expression I saw flicker in their depths.

"Sleep well?"

"Yes, thanks, though I didn't mean to sleep for such a long time. Someone should have awakened me. Is Charity annoyed? That is, any more than she already was?"

"You'll have to ask her." He answered rather harshly and moved past me.

"Jonas? Why are you all against me here?"

He leaned against the banister and hooked a thumb in the waistband of his pants. "You've got it wrong, Lady Delores. You're your own worst enemy."

"I beg your pardon?"

"I said, you're your own worst enemy. No one needs to be against you when you do the job so well yourself."

I stood on the steps a long while after he had clomped away. His opinion really mattered next to nothing. Who did he think he was, anyway?

I found Charity in the kitchen, and despite my resolve to maintain the upper hand with her, I felt a twinge of guilt at her appearance. She looked work-worn—run off her feet, and it was apparent that while I'd rested the day away, she'd continued to work. But after all, this inn was her responsibility, not mine.

"I'm reporting to work." I tried to make it a joke, but she

didn't smile. "What would you like me to do?"

"Sit down, cousin. Relax."

"But I mean it, Charity. I feel mountains better, and I'd like to dig in and help. I'll even clean if you really want me to. Surely housework can't be that difficult." She said nothing at that. "Or I could help with the cooking—I have done some cooking—actually I'm rather good." It was a lie. I'd never cooked anything much.

"Your return ticket is there on the table. I suggest you enjoy your first and last evening here. Oh, and Mama's awake now. She's asked to see you before you go."

"Before I go? You're kicking me out and Clara approves?"

"She knows I haven't much choice."

"Why? Simply because I insisted on a bath and a nap?"

"A nap? Is that what you call it? Look, I'm sorry, but I've too much to worry about without being saddled with a pampered—with a girl who hasn't the vaguest notion of what our life here is all about."

I took a gulp and tossed aside my pride. I couldn't go home—not like this! *I'd never live it down.* "Charity, please give me a chance, please! Oh, cousin, I'm in a spot. It would mean everything if you'd let me stay. There's a lot I can do. I'm . . . I'm educated!"

She refused to meet my gaze. "Look, I'm tired, and Mama won't be awake long. Why don't you go have a visit with her. It might be your last opportunity."

"Charity, why? Do you dislike me or something?" She continued with her cooking chores and was no longer even listening. "Charity?"

I left her to find Clara's room and collided with two sandy-haired children—a boy and a girl coming in the front door.

"Are you Delores Lyn?" the boy asked. I guessed they were Charity's children.

"I'm Mara and this is Aldan. We're both six. We're twins—not identical though."

"Excuse me." I forced my fixed smile to widen. "I'd love to visit with you, but later, all right?"

"You crying, Delores Lyn?" Mara's mouth opened in astonishment.

"Your mother's in the kitchen right now. Go on, will you?" I couldn't talk anymore—neither was it the time to see cousin Clara. I turned toward the stairs, but seeing Jonas's legs descending I pushed past the children and out the front door.

"Where're you going?" the children chimed together. "Hey, wait. Delores Lyn! Let us come, too!"

I hurried my pace, wishing that I could stop the tearing ache inside me. I hadn't wanted to come here in the first place, and so it could hardly matter that I wasn't to be allowed to stay. Besides, I was a grown woman, and just because this option had been cut off was no reason to fall apart. I could find work somewhere, and—

A screeching howl cut across my mental arguments. I turned to see Mara several yards behind me on her knees with Aldan hovering over her. She'd fallen, and there was nothing to do but stop and help.

"Well, are you hurt?" I asked with undisguised impatience. She only cried louder.

"Why wouldn't you wait up for us?" Aldan scolded in a tone very much like his mother's.

"Look, I told you I couldn't talk right now!" But I stooped down beside her and took her small foot in my hand. The ankle seemed perfectly fine to me.

"We wanted to come," Mara sniveled. "We wanted to come." Her crying was mostly histrionics, but no matter how I tried to reason, she wouldn't be soothed.

"Could I help, Princess?" It was Jonas Luker. I wouldn't meet his gaze. I'd had enough of him to last a good long time.

Aldan immediately started to tattle. Mr. Luker squatted and listened to the children recite their complaints as if everything they said could be given complete credence.

"Well?" He turned in my direction and waited, for an explanation from me, I suppose.

I smoothed a hand over my hair and then, realizing that I'd run out without discarding my apron, felt the color rise in my neck. To go out on a public street wearing an apron! I hastily untied it and placed it over my arm.

"Why didn't you wait for the children? It might have been a small way of helping their mother out!"

"I'd already told them no, that we'd talk later." I gave each child a stern shake of my finger. "They just wouldn't listen."

"Mara, I think your ankle's better now." He kissed her cheek and helped her up. "You and Aldan run and tell your mother we'll both be right there."

Without argument the two forgot the injury and were off like a shot.

"So where do you think you were going, anyway?"

I opened my mouth for an indignant reply, but was caught short. My hands went to the base of my throat as I looked about me. Where might I have been heading? The white spires of the temple caught my eye, and I waved a hand at them.

"Down there." My tone implied that it was none of his business. "I was going to see the temple grounds. I was here once before, you see, and never got the chance to look at the temple very closely. The architecture is, I understand, unique." I finished with what I knew was my most stunning smile. Men were such simple creatures really, and except for Papa, I'd never met a man who couldn't be wheedled out of a bad mood with some skillful coquetry. "Now if you'll excuse me—"

He swore then—a mild oath, but nevertheless the blood in my veins froze. It was the last straw. Insulted that he should use such language with me, I launched into my own attack.

"Mr. Luker, you seem to have yourself firmly entrenched into Clara Casston's affairs, and Charity's as well. But *do not* assume you can extend those same liberties to me. What I do here is none of your business!"

"You were sent here to *work*, and that certainly is my business."

"Oh? You think being a boarder gives you some right to interfere in a family—"

"As your *employer*, yes, I have the responsibility to do just that."

"Employer?" He was going too fast for me. Employer? Was he a hired manager of sorts? A partner maybe?

"Have you even lent a finger to help out here? This is your family! You know Clarey's ill, and you know how very much Charity needs your help, but no, you insist on a long leisurely bath, sleep the rest of the day away, then spruce up like some social butterfly and go off *sight-seeing!*"

"But it isn't that way—"

"Shut up and listen. Clarey has been asking for you all day. She's concerned about you. Do you understand how that might feel, to be concerned with someone other than yourself?"

"But why didn't Charity tell me?"

"She did! She specifically asked you to look in on Clarey, but what did you do? Run off to do your own selfish pleasure. What kind of a self-centered little nobody are you, anyway?" He gave me a hard shake and released me with such force my head snapped back in a painful jerk.

I hit him full in the face, flinching in case he retaliated. Instead, he turned on his heel and left me with my hand stinging and the horrible realization that I'd just slapped the only person who could conceivably override Charity's authority. If he were a partner, he could allow me to stay on.

"Jonas, wait! Listen, please." I chased along after him. "I didn't realize Clara had been *waiting* to see me. I was going to go see her, I was—but when I found out I'd be going back home in the morning I was so crushed—"

"You're going home already?" He stopped and looked at me.

"Hasn't Charity told you, then?"

His eyes glinted with exasperation. "You know she hasn't or I wouldn't be asking. I understood you'd come down here to help. Are you backing out now that you see it won't be a picnic?"

"This is Charity's decision, Mr. Luker. And I must abide by it, though I'd much rather stay. I did have my heart set on learning some more—more domestic responsibilities. You see, my talents—"

"Skip it. When did Charity decide this?"

"This afternoon, I think. I'm not sure; but she means it. She's even bought me passage to the train. She's explained that she just doesn't have the time to work with me. Of course, I quite understand. It's a disappointment, but if I'm at all underfoot then I must remove myself."

"How good of you." His tone was peculiar, and I wasn't sure if he believed me or not. "Your father won't be happy to see you, will he?"

I tried not to think of Papa's last words to me. *"Don't shame me again, Delores Lyn."*

"No." I forced the corners of my mouth upward. "It's true Papa and I have had a falling out, but I am his daughter. We've always been close. He'll understand." It was perhaps the worst falsehood I'd told, but I would not admit to anyone how bad things were—admit that if I went home now, it would finish my relationship with Papa for good. While he'd never really given me much attention, he had usually given me my own way. But those days were gone. I now knew Papa came just short of despising me. Why else had he written everything to Charity?

"You sound very sure of your father." He hadn't believed me.

"I am!"

He shook his head and ran a hand through the mane of black hair. "It's a pity you haven't learned to be more truthful. I might then be tempted to help you out."

I blinked at the criticism. "You think I'm lying?"

"I know you are. I've seen the letter. I know all about your irresponsible behavior with Mr. Stone. You'd been engaged a year and didn't think to be honest with him until a week or so before the scheduled ceremony. Isn't that correct? You weasled your way into his affections and those of his children with no intention of going through with it."

"That isn't exactly how it was." He made it sound so malicious.

"Oh, no?"

I didn't like his smile, but there was no use explaining, even if I could. Jonas Luker would hardly see my side of it—not when no one else had.

I turned back toward the inn, trying not to run. So Mr. Luker knew everything too. But he didn't. He didn't! No one did—only Grandmother, and she was gone.

I owed her everything. She had been my champion—my friend. I'd had to accept Egan, hadn't I? What else could I have done when she'd been humiliated because of me?

"But Delores, doesn't all this talk about Mark Staaton jilting you hurt?" Grandmother had said. "I, for one, find it singularly embarrassing. Worse—oh, my dear, I went to a great amount of trouble and expense to hire Mark and bring him to Ashley for you. What a laugh everyone's having on me now that he's married that Carrow girl instead. So think, *think*, for my sake as well as your own. Egan is heaven sent. He's rich; attractive in his way; older, true, but a proper match. What will it cost you to wear that fine ring of his for a little while? You'll boost his stodgy image and at the same time hush the gossipers. Then in time I'll find a clever way of breaking it off painlessly—I promise—for *both* of you, and everything will be fine again. Trust me, my dear. You must trust me."

33

Had Rachael lived it would have worked out flawlessly. She had a talent for making life march to her tune. It was a pity I hadn't the same gift.

Maybe it was better to be leaving Cottonstreet. With everyone thinking such things about me, it was almost a blessing to be forced out—almost.

FOUR

"There you are at last! Come in! Come in!" Clarey raised herself up on the pillows with apparent effort, and a smile lighted her surprisingly pale features. She'd always been brown from the sun, slim and full of a vigor that made one forget how small she was. Her dark hair was dusted with gray now, and her lovely features were so pinched that she seemed years older. Papa's favorite cousin. I had to study her a moment to be sure it was really her. "Close the door, will you?"

I did as she'd instructed and sat beside her. "You're ill—"

"Oh, no, not ill. It's just this confounded leg again. You remember it kept me from Aunt Rachael's funeral. It's been a trouble since I cut it—never heals up right."

Six or more months ago she'd been weeding with a scythe and had sliced the calf of her leg clean through. "I've done it though, this time." She winced as she shifted her leg to a more comfortable position. "Fell against it last week and broke it back open. Dr. Hallum says it's infected, and if I'm not careful I could lose it."

"Clarey! You should have telegrammed, and we wouldn't have come!"

35

She lay back, moving her head from side to side. "But I thought I'd be up and about long before now. You know doctors. They always tell you the worst, and Hal is no different. But I should have telegrammed you just the same. Then this marriage of Debra's would never have happened." The widely spaced eyes that so plainly labeled her an Ashley reddened with tears. "I saw Debra last night. Even she seemed unsure. Your father will blame me. I should never have asked Mel to look you up and ride down with you, but I was trying to help. There have been robberies in years past, and an escort seemed to be a good idea. How was I to know—"

"You couldn't! None of us could. Now don't worry about it, Clarey, please. If Papa blames anyone at all, it will be me. I did my best to encourage her to come."

"Forgive me, Delores, but when you realized Debra's intentions, why didn't *you* stop her?"

"I tried. I talked myself blue, honestly, but by then it was too late. She was enamored with him." To tell the truth, I hadn't even seen it coming. Mel had taken to Debra on our introduction to him at Ashley Heights a week before our departure, but I'd been so tied up with my own miseries that I'd been almost grateful to Mr. Stubbs for diverting my sister's attentions from me.

"I've been composing a letter here." Clara waved at a stack of papers on the table near the bed. "You can take it back with you in the morning. It should explain things and help Daniel understand this better. Oh, my—" She colored, and I knew she was thinking of the awkward situation between Charity and myself. Unlike her daughter, Clara had Grandmother Rachael's respect for delicacy, and though she knew of my recent troubles, Clara would, out of courtesy, never allude to them. "Your father needn't know you and Charity didn't get on. I'll simply tell him that with my leg and all I can't have you stay right now. That sounds plausible, don't you think?"

I didn't think so, but I nodded just the same. Papa would expect me to stay and help if things were so bad that Clarey was bedridden. But I appreciated Clara's consideration. It was a shame things hadn't worked out as at first planned. She'd been so thrilled at the prospect of having me down, had painted the life here in such a rosy light that I had almost deluded myself into believing that life at the inn would be quite an adventure. It had been her glowing, almost romantic letters that made Debra envious enough to insist that she come too.

"We've one problem though." Clarey became suddenly brisk. "There hasn't been time to find someone to accompany you back."

"Oh, don't worry about that. I've been on my own before."

"But traveling—"

"Oh, I've traveled alone many times. Papa may not know it, but I have. Besides, that's rather an old-fashioned idea anyhow."

She was shaking her head, and I tried again. I had to be allowed to leave alone. I hadn't any intention of going home, and a traveling companion would only be in the way.

"Clarey, I do appreciate it, but I'm nearly twenty-three years old, and with everything else you have to worry about, I prefer to go on my own."

"But if something should happen to you, my dear—"

"Nothing will, goodness!" I couldn't say anything about looking for employment. The knowledge would only put her in a tizzy. I could write and tell her where I'd found a position *after* I was settled. Because she seemed about to pursue the matter I changed the subject.

"Clarey, I've discovered something that disturbs me."
"Oh?"

"This Jonas Luker—he tells me he's your partner or something." Her look of concern melted into a smile.

"He said that? That he was my partner?"

"Well, something like that. Is it true?"

She shook her head. "No, not remotely."

I knew it! This inn belonged to Clarey, and the only real power here was Clarey. And here I'd appealed to Jonas Luker to help me. How degrading!

"Jonas is Sam's boy. You remember Sam, don't you? My husband and Sam's older boys built this guesthouse together. In fact, you should remember Jonas, too. Jonas was living here when you all visited that time just before Charity's marriage."

"He was?" I thought a moment of Jonas Luker's bronzed face and tall, big frame. I'd never seen him before, I was certain of it.

"Oh, yes. Jonas has lived here since he was a child."

"I didn't know that! I remember vaguely that you'd taken in a Lamanite child, but—" I stopped at Clarey's laughter.

"Taken in? Oh, you *have* been misinformed! I suppose it made Daniel and Rachael feel better to think I was helping out Sam, but in truth it's the other way around. This building belongs to the Luker family, Delores. I've simply managed it for them all these years."

It wasn't possible. "Jonas Luker owns *your* guesthouse?"

"Along with his brothers, yes. I'm almost certain you met him on your first stay here. But then, he's always on the run between here and Pine Valley, so maybe you didn't actually meet."

"He's—he's a very different kind of a fellow. I would have remembered him."

She laughed. "Maybe not, my dear. You seemed awfully taken with Charity's beau, as I remember, and Randall's the sort to notice attention from a stunning creature like you."

38   "Clarey, I was fourteen—a little girl!"

"But beautiful even then. You never go unnoticed, Delores Lyn, not in the biggest crowd. You look like Aunt Rachael all over again."

"I've been told that a lot, but especially by Grandmother herself."

Clarey laughed and reached out to squeeze my hand. "And I understand you miss her terribly."

"She was my dearest friend. When she was alive my life had order, structure, meaning—and ever since her death it's been chaos."

"She was a good woman, it's true." Cousin Clara frowned as though she were about to venture something I might not like, and I steeled myself for it. "Your father seems to think that Rachael never gave you much opportunity to learn—"

"Grandmother was always teaching me!"

"No, no. Let me finish. I was saying she didn't give you the chance to learn about life and what you really wanted for yourself. She was so domineering, not so much with your sisters as with you. And don't you think it was because she saw herself in you? She loved you, but it couldn't have been good for you having her live your life for you like that."

"It isn't true. I've been lost without her!"

"Yes, I know. But now you can find your own way. That's the way it's supposed to be, my dear. This may sound cruel, but as far as you're concerned, Rachael's passing has been a mixed blessing, and—"

I shot to my feet. "I could never consider losing Grandmother a blessing, cousin. She was not in the least bit domineering. She was strong and good, and she loved me. I know she loved me! You've been reading too much into what Papa says."

"Yes, maybe so. Forgive me." She patted the chair for me to sit down again. "It's a credit to you that you're so loyal to her memory, but then as I recall, you always have been committed to those you love."

"Have I?" I sank back into my chair. The compliment was so unexpected after the assault on Grandmother Rachael that I was absurdly grateful to Clara for having said it, true or not. "Have I really, cousin? You're not just saying that?"

"Even as a child, you'd fight like a tigress for your sisters or your father or Grandmother. Loyalty's a most admirable trait, Delores. We see far too little of it these days."

The remaining minutes of my visit with Clarey were so uplifting that when little Mara came to invite me into the dining room for supper, I dreaded leaving the fragile glow we'd created. "Maybe I could eat in here tonight, Clarey? I'd like to have as much time to talk with you as I can and—"

"Oh, no. I want you to have a chance to visit with the others, too."

"I'd rather not."

"Cheer up, Delores. You'll decorate the table in that gorgeous green gown. I can't deprive my boarders of that! But please look in on me before going up to bed, all right?"

I entered the dining room and stopped short. An old, white-haired man was in the midst of saying the blessing on the food. But even after he'd finished I hugged the door, uncertain as to where I should sit. It wasn't that the immense table was crowded—it could easily seat twenty-five or more people and tonight the group was sparse, but I felt so much an outsider. At the far end Charity sat with her children, one on either side of her. Several empty places separated Aldan from Jonas. At the other end were two fussily dressed women I hadn't seen before. Both were elderly, and both were heavily involved in their own conversation.

"Oh, *there* you are!" Charity looked up and spied me hovering half in and half out of the room, and I was glad for the hum of voices that helped mask her aggrieved tone. "I was beginning to think you didn't need food to survive. As far as I know, you haven't had a thing to eat since you arrived, have you?"

I shook my head. The last mouthful I'd eaten had been at the camp in the dawn hours—Thelma Sackett's greased eggs, and they'd been abominable.

"Well, find a place!" She gave no more help than that

and turned to assist her children in filling their plates.

"Miss Ashley, would you like to sit with me?" I turned and realized it was the older man who had offered the blessing on the food who had spoken. He smiled and touched the back of the chair next to him. I appreciated the gesture and accepted it even though he was sitting facing Jonas Luker. But it seemed that Jonas meant to ignore me. He hadn't so much as looked my way.

"Miss Ashley, I'm Alexander Wubbleton. And may I introduce the Reiley sisters—" Mr. Wubbleton nodded to the two older women I passed as I moved up the table.

"Hello, I'm Esther and this is Lyddie."

"Yes, and you're Clarey's lovely cousin we've heard so much about."

"Thank you. I'm Delores. Do you board here?" I extended my hand to each of them.

"Have for better than a year now," the most outrageously dressed one answered, the one who'd been identified as Lyddie. "We like being out of the city center, and we're closer to the temple here."

I smiled and slipped into my chair next to Mr. Wubbleton. "It's very pleasant meeting you both."

"Esther and I look forward to hearing you play, don't we, Esther?"

"And sing, too. Clarey's told us all how well you sing!"

We all nodded and smiled again with the awkwardness one feels upon introductions, and I turned to inspect the food. My side vision showed Jonas's eyes on me, and I felt the muscles in the back of my neck tighten at the strain in the air. If I hadn't been so hungry, I would have skipped the meal altogether and stayed in my tiny room. But my stomach was giving little choice—it was eat or faint.

41

With bowed head I busied myself with eating. Conversation between Jonas and Mr. Wubbleton resumed, and I relaxed a little and began to taste the food. It was simpler than I was used to, but pleasant, and I could trust that it had been prepared in sanitary conditions, which hadn't been the case with much of what I'd been forced to eat since leaving home. Once I'd started to eat, I realized how famished I'd been. I couldn't seem to get enough.

"My, my." Mr. Wubbleton was chuckling next to me. "Such a slim little thing you are, and yet what an appetite. It's nice to see a girl tuck into her food like that."

I regretted the shift of attention, and smoothing a napkin over my mouth answered in a low tone, "Forgive me, I'm not usually so starved."

"I take it your trip down was difficult?"

"Not really—"

"Ah hah! You don't want to talk about the shivaree party, I take it?"

"So you know about that?"

He laughed. "Oh, I'd like to. Melvin and your sister were here for a while last night. Young Melvin seemed pleased as pudding with himself, but not your sister. She was white as a sheet and very worried about you."

"Yes, my sister can be easily led, but she's a dear just the same. I wish I could say good-bye to her before I leave."

"Leave?" Alexander Wubbleton nudged my shoulder, and I realized too late I'd spoken my thoughts aloud. "You're going back already?"

I nodded. "Isn't the food delicious? I've always loved young peas."

I saw questions forming in the old man's eyes and struggled to think of a way to get him to drop the subject.

"Do you think these peas were grown here in the garden, Mr. Wubbleton?"

"Isn't it awfully soon to be going already? I mean you've only arrived, and I understood that you would be working here with Charity."

"Yes, I know. I really would like to stay, Mr. Wubbleton, but it seems it just isn't possible."

The man was sensitive enough to see I didn't want to explain. "So, you're going in the morning. Pity—Clarey's talked about your coming for weeks. She has a great admiration for you, Miss Ashley. She said you were first and always a lady, poised and charming. It's true. And I must say it does my failing eyesight good just to look at you!"

Jonas's sudden snort of laughter caught me off guard, and I lifted my eyes in surprise.

"Wubbles, old friend—" He rocked back in his chair, his narrowed eyes not leaving my face. "This lady, *this lady,* might have fooled even you last night. She wanted to scratch my eyes out just for offering her some supper."

"Then my admiration is doubled," the old gentleman put in gallantly. "She's got spirit to match the flaming glory of her hair."

Defeated, Jonas Luker only grunted and went back to his meat.

"Tell me, since you're returning immediately to Ogden, would you mind carrying a letter with you? I have an agent there who's trying to sell some land for me. A Mr. Neason." He paused to clear his throat, and I took the opportunity to make my situation clearer.

"Mr. Wubbleton, you must know I'd be most happy to do that for you, but . . ." I hesitated, unsure of the wisdom of disclosing my plans to look for a position. If word were to get to Clarey . . .

"I'm imposing then!" He put up a hand. "You needn't worry about it. I'll simply post it tomorrow."

"I'll help you take care of your letter, Wubbles," Jonas muttered to his plate. It was that rolling disgust in his voice that decided me.

"Yes, perhaps you would do that for this dear gentleman, Mr. Luker. Inasmuch as I'm not going to Ogden, I couldn't very well take it there for him." I turned back to Mr. Wubbleton. "My plans you see, sir, are to find employment in Milford or Leamington or—I don't know, but in one of those little towns."

Jonas Luker's head shot up, and I had the satisfaction of seeing his brow wrinkle in disapproval. "If you go in the morning, you're going all the way back to Ogden Hole and your father in Ashley Valley!"

"If?" I challenged with a cool smile. "I thought there was no disputing the matter, and since you've all decided, I've made a decision of my own. I want to work. I've come here to work, and since I can't do that now, I'll simply go somewhere else and do it."

"You want to work!" Jonas threw down his napkin.

"Yes, I do. I'll teach school, I think, providing of course that I find a position."

"Is this wise, Miss Ashley?" Mr. Wubbleton broke in. "Shouldn't you remain here until you've positively secured something? Your plans sound vague, and I don't think it's safe for a young thing like you to just—"

"Not at all. Not at all safe!" It was Lyddie Reiley, speaking in a strident voice from her end of the table. She was shaking her fork at me, and the yellow-gray locks above her brow bounced furiously. "You tell her, Essie. You tell her about that Thorpe woman. What was her name? You know, Hy's daughter."

"Amelia Thorpe, Lyddie, but I don't think we should be interrupting. It isn't polite. Excuse us, please." The younger of the two women smiled in apology and resumed eating.

"Bah, it's our duty to tell her." Lyddie Reiley was not one to be silenced easily. "This Amelia was a pretty thing—like you—and she went traveling about as free as the wind, and the most tragic thing happened to her." The waving fork halted in midair and fell with a clatter to her plate.

44   "Lyddie, hush!"

"Disappeared, she did. And when she surfaced again she was with Ike and Noah Strong, them outlaws from Colorado. Her family said she never went willingly—at least not in the beginning. Now that's a fate worse than death, but I can tell you about one o' those too—a death, I mean. Ceil Jergie was on her way to work in the Arizona Strip. Never arrived."

"Lyddie, this is not a subject for the dinner table."

"Essie, I'm merely trying to point out—"

"You'll alarm the children, sister!"

A gasp from Charity hushed both Reiley women, and all eyes turned to the opposite end of the table where my cousin sat staring in horror out the window. After some tense seconds, she broke her frigid pose, pushed back her chair, and stood.

"See what you've done," Esther began. But it hadn't been the story. Even with Charity's breathless instructions to the children to finish up on their own, her eyes were still fastened on the window, and I strained to see what it was outside that had alarmed her.

Jonas moved to her side, and there was a muffled exchange of words. "We'll take care of it, Char. You haven't had a chance to eat. Lady Delores there will help out, won't you, Lady D? You're finished."

"Help out?"

"That's right. Come along, and hurry!" He disappeared into the kitchen.

His request had been more like an order, and I came close to staying right where I was, but then I thought of Clarey. Perhaps she needed something. I nodded to the women and Mr. Wubbleton and followed in Jonas Luker's wake. It would, after all, be churlish to refuse to help dear Clara no matter how abominably these two had treated me.

"And don't leave the door standing open." Jonas spoke with impatience from the doorway off the kitchen that led to the back staircase.

Still grudging, I turned back to obey when a stir at the table caused me to pause. The Reiley women were fanning themselves with excitement and twittering like schoolgirls, and Charity had pasted a luminous smile on her mouth and was moving to the entry to meet an incoming guest with a greeting so effusive I wouldn't have believed it if I hadn't seen it myself. But then, as the gentleman moved into my line of vision, I understood. His arrival had set the calm dinner hour on its end because he was a man to be reckoned with. Everything about him spoke of power.

"Lady, shut that door and come on!"

"I'll be right there, Mr. Luker." I waved, shushing him, for the sight of the tall stranger was so arresting I couldn't help staring. He was lean in an aristocratic way, with thick, well-trimmed brownish hair that had gone quite silver at each temple, and his handsome features were more than memorable. His face, though clean-cut and sensitive, had a hardness about it that I liked. It was as if he'd seen the world and knew his way around it. And the man had *money*. It was in his bearing—in the expensive cut of his clothing. Though his suit was covered with dust, he wore it like a prince.

"Who is he?" I asked, impressed that such a man would be here in remote St. George, of all places.

Jonas exhaled sharply, strode back, and shut the door himself before taking my wrist in hand. "Lady, you're a lotta help, you know that?"

"I just want to know who—"

"Miles Lassiter, all right?" He spoke with a disgust that seemed to include us both—the man Lassiter and myself, but I didn't care and spoke the name softly to myself as Jonas tugged me after him up the circular staircase. *Miles Lassiter. Miles Lassiter.*

Now there was a man! I wanted to ask if he was by any chance single, but anticipating Jonas's reaction, thought better of it.

We'd no sooner emerged into the upstairs hallway when Jonas was telling me to hurry back and bring a broom. "And a dusting bin, too," he barked, and then he disappeared back into the nearest front bedroom. The door stood open, and a stream of light fell into the dimly lit corridor.

I frowned back into the shadowy staircase below. The steps were steep and descended in a tight and difficult spiral. If I had to go back down again, then I was taking the front stairs. What was all the fuss about anyway?

"Mr. Luker, what is wrong here?" I stepped into the room and stopped short at the sight of the spacious luxury that I'd been denied—half was in perfect order and half was littered with overturned furniture and the contents of opened drawers. Books and papers were strewn across the impressive bed and bright floor rugs. A basin had been broken, and glass was scattered over everything. "Oh, dear, what ever happened here?"

Jonas was shoving books like mad back onto their shelves, and he didn't pause in his task as he answered. "Meg, our cook, tender-hearted and trusting, let a cattleman in here. This is Lassiter's room—Clarey's biggest customer. Do I need to tell you he won't like it? Now, are you going to help or not?"

I began to snatch up the papers. "But we'll never get this done before he comes up. Is that the idea?"

"Charity's going to delay him. Just work, will you? And where is that broom?" Jonas slammed another book into place and stood. "Never mind, I'll get it. Just hurry with those papers. What a fine time he's picked to come back."

"But why would someone do such a thing? It looks deliberate to me."

Jonas shrugged and righted a chair on his way out. "Who knows? Miles Lassiter is an outside investor—brings sheep in from California and buys up tracts of mountain land to graze them on. There's a lot that don't like him much." From his tone I gathered that he placed himself in that category. He was gone, and, hoping to impress him with my efficiency on his return, I flew through the papers, doing my best to avoid the jagged edges of glass sifted

47

throughout. I was very nearly done when he came back into the room, closing the door with a resounding slam. I looked up, but instead of seeing Jonas swooping down behind me, it was Lassiter!

"Thief! What did you think you would find?" His hand came out and hit my wrist against the floor, forcing me to drop the bundle of papers. Simultaneously a fiery pain shot along my arm. Glass—I could feel it cutting my skin beneath the pressure of Miles Lassiter's hold.

"My hand—" I tried to tell him, but he wouldn't listen. He continued to press my wrist, and the glass shard sawed deeper.

"Who sent you here? Cattlemen? You can tell them for me the deal's gone through. It's too late. I own the Mayatuck and no map will—"

"Mr. Lassiter, let me go! It's not what you think!"

He shifted his hand slightly, lessening the pressure. "Listen to me, girl—"

"I don't know anything about any map, nor am I here to do you harm."

His laugh was unpleasant, and I struggled to make him lose his grip. It was a mistake—again he drove the hand unmercifully to the floor. *Jonas. Where was Jonas?*

"So, you just happen to be innocently going through my things? I'm back early and you thought—"

"No, no. It isn't like that, I tell you. I'm cleaning. And you're hurting my hand. It's cut, can't you see?" My voice rose when he still wouldn't listen to reason. "Mr. Lassiter, I don't care if you are cousin Clarey's best customer, you have no right to treat me like this. Now let me go. You can clean up this mess yourself for all I care!"

He moved around to better see my face. "You're a cousin to Clara Casston?" Disbelief glinted in his narrowing eyes.

"Yes, and my hand is killing me. It's cut, I tell you, and if you don't let me up, I shall start screaming!"

His gaze shifted to the hand still pressed to the floor. A

bright smear of red had blotched the nearest paper. With an expletive of surprise he lifted my hand to see blood trickle in a tiny stream down my arm. "It's not much more than a graze." He refused to feel remorse.

"It's much more than that. It's frightfully painful. The glass is still in it."

"So what are you doing in my room?"

"I told you; I'm cleaning it. It needs it, wouldn't you say?" He laughed then and let me go.

"If you're a maid here, I'll eat my hat."

"I'm not a maid," I said, feeling offended at the label.

"You're not? You're cleaning, but you don't work here?" He was shaking his head with amusement, and I realized I hadn't made myself very clear.

"Mr. Lassiter, I'm Clara's cousin, Delores Lyn Ashley. Your room was vandalized, and I was asked to restore it to some order. Clara's ill, and I came here to help out. I was doing this as a favor to her."

He bent toward me, his face intent. "This is the truth?" he asked softly.

"Go ask Clara or Charity! Now, if you'll excuse me, I'd like to see to my hand."

He stepped into my path and, searching inside his vest pocket, brought out a spotless square of pressed linen. "You may use my handkerchief if it will help."

"No, thank you." I was cross now as I swept around him to the door and angry at myself for having been so attracted to him in the first place.

"But you're going to soil your lovely dress, look!" He moved and wrapped the cloth loosely about the wound. "And you'll need some assistance to remove the glass."

"You've done quite enough already, Mr. Lassiter!" I swept out of the room then, nearly colliding with Jonas. It was about time! I wanted to storm at him, but my wrist protested. It needed to be taken care of immediately.

* * * * *

"Well, you've got your own way. Are you proud of yourself?" Charity had come to my room with a fresh pitcher of water and a tray of clean bandages. "You really are like Rachael, aren't you!"

"What do you mean?"

"Forever innocent. Oh, Delores Lyn, I'm one person you can't fool with your pretty green eyes. I know how you wrangled Miles into speaking up for you with Jonas." She crossed to the bed and stared down at my clumsily wrapped wrist. "So you had an accident? Are you sure that too wasn't planned?"

"Charity, this day comes close to being the worst of my life. I'm tired of your bullying. I look forward to leaving in the morning."

"But you're not leaving, and you know it!"

"I'm not?" I opened my eyes to see her glowering over me.

"Jonas tells me he explained your presence to Miles Lassiter, told him you'd been fired and were leaving first thing tomorrow. And guess what? Our rich patron has taken a liking to you. Isn't that odd? Instead of tearing at us for letting someone in his room, he's on bended knee for having hurt your hand. He insists he make it up to you. So you're to stay. Surprised?"

"Very." I was. It was more than I'd hoped for—now there'd be no searching about in unfamiliar towns for work. I could stay until I'd mended my bridges with Papa, and when I returned, it wouldn't be with more mud on my face.

"You planned this, cousin. Don't deny it. But I'm going to make you a promise. I'll show you no special treatment here. I expect the same quality of work from you as I do from everyone else. You will be up at five o'clock with the rest of us and work until the work is done—which it never is. Jonas has told me you must have a day off—Tuesdays are slow, and when they are, you may have that to yourself."

"And Sundays? Surely we don't work on the Sabbath!"

Charity's smile wasn't reassuring. "We work doubly hard on Saturday to prepare for Sunday. Usually we can attend church and have a comparatively leisurely afternoon, but the dawn hours are filled with feeding the guests, cleaning up afterward, straightening rooms, and last-minute baths. The other two meals are light, and the food is set out so the guests can serve themselves. We may see little rest, but we do our best to honor the Lord's day."

My future was suddenly less bright than it had seemed a few moments before.

"I'll see you in the morning—five o'clock sharp!"

"I'm not sure I can wake up that early on my own, Charity; I'm not used to it."

"Don't worry, cousin. I'll knock, and knock, and shake you out if necessary. Well, then—" She sighed and turned toward the door, only to stop midway. "You haven't done a very good job with that bandage. Would you like me to redo it for you?"

"It's fine."

She shrugged and, leaving the water and muslin strips on the bureau, went out.

FIVE

The next morning I found myself assigned to the kitchen. "As you told me you do cook, it seemed the best place to start you," Charity explained. "We'll have Meg here to help you a lot of the time. The two of you should manage all right, and one of her girls—Trudy or Aimee—could help wash up on the heaviest days. Oh—Mama likes to help with menu suggestions. She needs something to think about, so do check with her daily." She left me, assuming I'd take over the cooking.

"I'm Meg Gibbons. I live around the corner and come in now and then to help out." She dried her hands on her apron before taking mine.

She had a likable, matronly face, and her brown hair was old-fashioned and matched her stout little frame. She wore it poofed on the sides with a squat, fat bun on top.

Her smile was warm. "Don't mind Charity's impatience. Too much on her plate right now. Clara's been miserable with her poor leg. She's the worst patient in the world, and it's hard on Charity. Give her some time, and you'll like her."

"It isn't necessary that I like her, Meg, but I do appreciate your kindness."

It seemed I'd said the wrong thing, for a shadow passed over her wide face; unsmiling, she turned back to the kettle heating on the huge iron stove. After a rather uncomfortable silence, I ventured to reinstate myself with the woman.

"How many children do you have, Meg?"

"Four." She didn't elaborate.

"Charity mentioned two girls—Trudy, and Aimee, was it? Any sons?"

"No, miss. They're all girls." Again silence.

Meg went about quietly working. I gave up trying to win her over and concentrated on my assignment. On the whole I was happy with it, and the title cook sat better with my pride than did scrubwoman or upstairs maid.

It wasn't long, though, before Meg saw I hadn't an idea in the world about preparing food properly, and I could see speculation in her eyes about my having lied to Charity. Finally, without my having to ask, she began to contribute to my meager knowledge with discreet suggestions like: "Vanilla, you add vanilla to cream."

"That's vinegar you're holding, isn't it?"

"Use a smaller knife when peeling so there'll be something left of the potato when you're through with it."

"Plain meat isn't a disaster, so don't fret. We'll scrap the gravy tonight, and no one need say a word to Charity."

By the Sunday evening of the first week I was nearly frantic. Meg encouraged me to look on the bright side as I blundered about, but I had to admit to myself that I'd never felt more inept or shamed. Who could have imagined *cooking* would be such a chore?

And what was worse, whenever Charity came in to check on each meal's progress, I turned all thumbs—knocking, spilling, dropping whatever I had in hand. But Grandmother would have been proud, for despite my lack of confidence, I kept my head determinedly high. It was difficult and at times bordered on the impossible, but I behaved as if I were a grand cook. If it hadn't been for the

53

sorry comments drifting from the dining room day after day, I might even have fooled someone.

On the weekends the inn filled up with boarders, many from the mines. Several objectionable men said whatever came to mind. One of them announced loudly one morning, "It's that new pretty girl what's wrecked our food. She must be family else whyn't they fire 'er?"

That very night Charity confronted me over a pot of scorched stew.

"I'm afraid, cousin, we can't continue to disappoint our patrons. You can't cook. I don't care what Meg says, you can't cook worth a darn!"

"But she's learning." Meg, bless her heart, was quick to my defense. She seemed to have forgiven my earlier comments about Charity.

"And in the meantime we're starving—all of us. Now Jonas agrees with me on this. The kitchen just isn't the place for Delores. I think she should switch with your Aimee and take the upstairs cleaning. Surely there's not much she could do wrong with making beds and doing floors. On lighter days she could pitch in and help with Mara and Aldan and maybe work in the garden some with Wubbles."

"Well, you're the boss, Charity, but I hardly think Aimee will solve our problems in here. Delores is being trained. She's bound to make a few mistakes. If we pull her out now, what have we accomplished? Now if I could help a little more with the cooking—"

"If you did *all* of the cooking, yes, that still leaves plenty for Delores, doesn't it? She can watch and learn and at the same time do the scrubbing up. That way she may gradually pick up cooking. I see what you mean."

54 "And would you?" Meg looked a little worried. "Would you do that—settle for scrubbing up and things?"

Charity whirled, raising skeptical brows. "Well?"

I looked at the clutter around me. In better than a week I hadn't washed a single dish. Meg had done it all. She hadn't minded—at least she'd never given any hint that she had. So maybe it wouldn't be such a miserable job. Of course, it wasn't what I wanted—a far cry from my longed-for hostess work. "I—I—" I looked from one to the other. "I've already written Papa that I'm, well, that I'm a cook here."

"So?" Charity refused to see my predicament. "Write him again and tell him you're now our chief dishwasher."

"Or perhaps you could say assistant cook. That does sound better, doesn't it?" Meg seemed to understand my need for a title I could live with. "Yes, that's true. You will be assisting the cook."

Charity didn't object, and I felt relieved that I'd no longer be expected to turn out each meal. For the first few days or so I was content watching while Meg stirred up very successful dishes. Everyone was happy with the change and said so again and again, which further hurt my pride, and I vowed to learn the skill of cooking as soon as possible and overwhelm the lot of them.

My most distasteful task was the pots. They were literally always before me. The hot water made the kitchen hotter than ever, and by the next weekend I began to believe that I'd truly landed myself in the most difficult job in the house. Aimee and Trudy were done with their cleaning and off and away before one o'clock, but I was a permanent fixture at the dishpan.

I soon learned I hadn't escaped the chore of scrubbing floors either. "Scrubbing up, " Charity insisted one night, "also means this floor. Look at this mess. Sweeping is not enough!" Resigned now to this menial work, I took the news without batting an eye, consoling myself that the kitchen wasn't as large as it might have been. But I was careful to undertake the job early in the morning so no one ever caught me down on my knees with a scrub brush in my hand.

I told myself repeatedly that anything was better than

being sent home to Papa shamed as I very nearly was, and remembering that, I did not complain. I came close to it, but then I could see that Charity and Jonas were waiting for me to do just that. Any excuse and I'd be off and gone! So I kept my mouth shut and plowed on. By the end of the third week my soft, long-nailed hands were a mess, the nails spoiled beyond repair and my skin roughened with a bumpy rash that thrived on water. It was impossible, I was finding, to keep myself looking attractive in the kitchen. In one way I hardly cared. It was as if I were suddenly another person. I was tired all the time, and the heat sapped my strength, and besides, who was there to impress?

Miles Lassiter had disappeared as abruptly as he'd come. Thank heaven for that. I couldn't have borne his seeing me slaving like a servant girl—especially after his courtly apology to me.

My first day in the kitchen he'd sought me out, his gaze moving over me as if he liked very much what he saw. He wanted us to be friends, he'd said, and the words had been spoken with a certain gleam in his eye. And then, later on that evening, he had offered me the use of his books and his reading chair while he was away.

"My business detains me for long periods of time. You might as well make use of my library. I have a chair there by the window, and in the mornings with the breeze blowing through, you'll find it more than comfortable."

I'd begun to protest, but he wouldn't hear of it. "Please." His fingers brushed my lips to silence them. "I would take it as a token of your kind forgiveness to me if you'll make use of my books and room anytime you wish. Please."

It was a daydream I indulged in many times thereafter. I would be sitting in the masculine luxury of Mr. Lassiter's room perusing tomes of Shakespeare or Dryden. Of course, I would be in one of my prettiest dresses, and, as I'd read, totally engrossed, the door would open. Startled, I would look up to see Miles bending over me, his eyes softening on my own . . .

But my waking hours were no longer mine, and there'd been little time to do anything other than dream while I scoured one dirty pot after another. I began to look for Miles Lassiter's return with something like longing.

Debra was horrified on her first visit to me. "Delores! Darling, what's happened? You look positively awful!"

I shoved my drooping hair away from my eyes and stepped back to see my sister standing in the dining-room doorway. It seemed months since I'd seen her, though it couldn't have been much more than three weeks. She'd sent little scribbled notes on her pink writing paper telling me how busy she was settling in and becoming a wife, but promising to come see me first chance she got. I'd expected some warning. It didn't help my sagging self-respect to be caught like this.

"Are you all right, Lori Lyn?" Her abrupt switch to my childhood name signaled true distress. "Have you been sick or something?" She ventured into the room careful not to touch anything with her pale lemon gloves. Her yellow swiss dress was new, her hair in an older upswept style. She looked radiant.

"No, Deb, I've just been working. Working over hot water. I suppose I'm flushed."

"Flushed? You look feverish and bedraggled, and— and—" She stopped, unaware that her comments had been far from cheering. "And thin. Oh, what are they doing to you here? How can Clara allow you to work so hard?"

"Clara, as you know, is sick, and please don't go pitying me, sister. You've simply caught me at a bad time." I moved to the sideboard to dry my hands and offered Debra a chair at the table. "Would you like a sugar cake?"

"Oh, it's much too hot to eat." She looked back out at the cheery dining room. "It's so dismal in here. Couldn't we sit out there for a moment and visit?"

57

"I suppose." We sat with the open windows fanning us, my newly married baby sister in her crisp, high-fashion clothes and glistening hair, and me in my limp colorless linen. My embarrassment made small talk difficult. I hoped this visit would be quick.

"So, tell me how've you been? Are you happy here?" She too seemed nervous.

"I'm fine, and yes—very." I looked down at my fingers and then, spying my rough skin and torn nails, pushed them beneath the table.

"I . . . I'm sorry about your getting shivareed like that. It wasn't fair of us not to tell you, Lori."

"Water under the bridge." The episode seemed ages ago, and I was too tired to care about anything that happened that far back.

"Yes, I know, but still I want you to understand that I was just terribly worried about you. Mel was too. We've bought you a little gift to patch things up. It isn't quite finished, but then you'll be glad of that."

"There's nothing to patch up, Deb. We're sisters."

"Please accept it, Lori." She jumped to her feet and rushed out into the entry, coming back with a large box in her hands. "This is to replace the dress that Connan spoiled. To be fair I should tell you he did give Mel a little money. Anyway, it's being made by the same woman who did this yellow one for me. Don't you love it?" She whirled about, showing it off. "And you wouldn't believe what a great price this was. But anyway, open yours. We hope you like it."

I did. Debra had good taste in clothes and an eye for what looked best on a person. She'd given me a light laven-58 der voile. It was one of my best colors, and the dress was fashionably cut with soft petaled sleeves and a sweetheart neckline. It would be cool and pretty to wear when it was finished. "It's very nice, Debra."

"You like it, don't you?"

"Yes, I do. I love it."

She giggled at my acceptance. "Oh, good. Then you need only go and have it fitted. Here's her card. She's just around the corner, and when it's all done, you're to wear it with us to the Social Hall or a play or something. And there's a dance coming up soon. Mel will fix you up with an escort. That might help cheer you a little, right?"

I smiled my appreciation. She was trying so hard. "Thanks Debra, really, but you don't have to keep trying to cheer me. I might not look it right now, but I'm fine. And please don't go trying to find me an escort. I'm perfectly able to get a man when I want one."

"Oh, I know, Delores, but working so much, who can you meet? Until you can be properly introduced around, you'd better let us help."

I laughed outright at that. "No, thanks, and besides, I won't have much time until Clarey's well."

"But that could take all summer. And you can't miss the dance. It's to be very soon, Melissa tells me."

"Melissa?"

"Mel's sister. She's sweet on Jonas, if you want to know—a real darling she is. She's like a little mother, even to her own mother, and she told me about a fellow who sounds right for you and—"

"No, Debra, no!" At her crestfallen look I added, "At least not until I give it a try myself, all right? Now tell me about *you*. Are you still in love? Is married life anything like you hoped it would be?"

"Better, Lori, better." That's all it took to get Debra safely onto another subject. We spent a good thirty minutes while she related the happy events of her first few married weeks. "The Stubbs are the dearest people, Delores. I love them already. You'll have to come and see me often. It's just an hour's walk from here, or perhaps Charity could let you borrow a buggy. Anyway, do you have any time off at all? They can't make you work *every* day, can they?"

59

"I have Tuesdays when we're not busy. And we're usually not."

"Good, come Tuesday then, will you? Let me draw you a map so you won't get lost."

She was just finishing up when we heard a scuffle of boots and looked up to see Jonas and Mel standing over us.

"Time to leave, hon." Mel grinned at his wife.

"I'm just inviting Delores over to see us Tuesday, Mel. She needs to do something fun, and I thought I could show her how our house is coming."

"Sure. Come on over." Mel's tone was unenthusiastic, and I noticed an odd look in his eyes as his gaze traveled over me.

I blushed at the memory of my unappetizing appearance. "I will if I can, thank you." I stood and glanced at Jonas Luker's compressed mouth. "I'd better get back to work now."

After they'd gone, Jonas found me back at my dishpan. "Where's Meg today?"

"She had to leave for a while. Her youngest is sick."

He leaned against the counter, his eyes on my profile. "And Charity? Where's she off to?"

"I don't know. Maybe in the office—maybe with Clarey." I finished the last of the utensils and started on the pans, but the water needed changing. I gripped the dishpan and began to lift it when Jonas took it from me.

"You ought to bail the water out. You'll break your back doing it that way. Here, I'll do it. Why don't you just sit down. You look like you could stand to."

As Jonas went outside with the full dishpan, I caught sight of the clock. I'd wasted an hour or more visiting with Debra. Meg could be back any moment to start supper, and I hadn't even cleaned up the noon meal completely. When Jonas returned to refill the pan with hot water from the reservoir, he began to help put the dishes away. It was such a change from his usual aloof behavior and a shock to see him actually working in a kitchen.

"You're doing all right here in the kitchen, aren't you, Lady D?"

"Fine."

He was silent a while longer as we worked together. "You don't mind cleaning up all the time?"

I reached for another pan and forced myself to say, "Not much."

"Good." His tone implied that he didn't believe what I'd said, but at the same time it had been what he wanted to hear. "Good," he echoed absently. "But even so—" He picked up a handful of spoons and threw them with a vengeance into the drawer. "You needn't make yourself a slave to this."

"I'm not!"

"Oh, no?" His gaze compelled mine to his. "Everyone else finds some time to themselves—even Charity, but you're always in here. You look dead on your feet today. What are you trying to prove?"

His censuring hurt. Far from being pleased at my efforts, he was angry. I couldn't understand why. I'd expected surprise or compliments at my ability to work so hard, but no!

"It isn't just coincidence, is it? Are you trying to get Debra's sympathy maybe? And make Charity and me look bad in the bargain?"

He was so far afield from my real intentions that I couldn't begin to defend myself. I felt wronged through.

"Maybe this kind of work *is* new to you. If you need help, why don't you ask for some. We could get Meg's girls to stay longer and—"

"Meg and I can get along fine," I mumbled, turning away from him. "I'm getting better at it, really. Today I'm slower. I don't know why. The heat, I guess. But I'm nearly finished, and before Meg gets back—before Meg gets back . . ." I heard a mournful whine outside that prompted me. "I'm taking Mr. Wubbleton's old dog for a walk." Except for going to church I hadn't been out of the inn. From

61

now on I'd change that. These people didn't appreciate my long hours anyway.

"Good." Jonas's voice rumbled behind me. "See that you do!"

Meg was back before I could leave, and I knew my walk would have to be forgone, but not so: "Jonas has given orders that you take a walk—a long walk. And if you come back too soon I'm not to let you in the kitchen!" Meg's smile was hiding something. "So be off with you!"

* * * * *

After a good wash, and with my hair brushed and re-done in a simple braid down my back, I put on a fresh, cream-colored cotton. Except for a standup, open-collared neckline, it was plain and light with a slimmer cut skirt, and I decided I'd even wear it to serve supper that night. Let it be stained and ruined. These days wouldn't go on forever, and at least I would look nice. Tonight I wasn't having Jonas or anybody else thinking I was after pity.

The dog was so pathetically thankful to have some attention he nearly had me dirty before I was out the gate. He bounded excitedly after me, yapping madly, paying no heed to my scolding him not to jump up and tear my skirt.

It was cooler now—nice for St. George. The houses and yards were well kept; many (along this street especially) were green fenced. *Green*—I wondered about that. It was unexpected.

The red hills to the north flamed brighter, and the black hills on the west cut a swathe of shadow knifestraight under the blazing fire that bathed the city. Some people might find such primitive scenes beautiful. But to me it was frightening, all this parched land stretching into hundreds of miles of nothingness on all sides. I determined again to leave it to Debra and my cousins as soon as I could and go home to Ashley.

On my return from my walk I was met by Alexander Wubbleton.

"What a thoughtful thing to do, miss. I thank you for thinking of my old dog. He gets little exercise with me these days."

"You're quite welcome, Mr. Wubbleton." I smiled, feeling refreshed and rested from my excursion.

"And I notice you giving him a bit of meat now and then. I'm grateful for that too. I know it troubles Miss Charity to see you doing it."

Still feeling the glow of my rest, I spoke impulsively and carelessly loud. "Charity's far too practical. And what's the harm of feeding a dog. He only takes scraps."

"Yes, scraps that could go to the pigs and chickens that yield something back to us. That dog doesn't do anything but *take!*" Charity had come from nowhere to confront the both of us. We endured an uneasy silence before Mr. Wubbleton spoke, his white head down. "Old Dog had his day, Miss Charity, when he was a big help to me."

"Oh, I'm sure of that, Wubbles, but that day has long since passed." Her tone had softened in partial understanding, but the words kept coming. "And look at the doors! We just had them painted this spring, and already that dog has scarred them up with his infernal pawing." Throwing up her hands she explained, "*Someone* must be practical around here or we'd all starve to death. This inn is supposed to be a paying enterprise. If it weren't for Jonas subsidizing us lately, we'd be out of business!" Shaking her head, she stalked away to her office.

"She's a worn-out little thing, she is," Mr. Wubbleton spoke in her defense at my glaring disapproval. "I remember the time when Miss Charity would have been the first to take in a stray. But life's been tough on her, it has."

63

* * * * *

I couldn't stand it. No matter what I tried I couldn't get to sleep nights—not until the early dawn hours, and then Charity was after me to get up. Despite my resolves, I wasn't sure I could go on like this—working all day and not sleeping at night. How did all the others stay in their hot little rooms and sleep? Thoughts of the cooler night air outside had me up and tugging at the coverlet on my bed. I moved quietly outside to the upper veranda and put my quilt down on a bench. With only a sheet over me, I closed my eyes to the cool, blissful darkness.

Sleeping outside would have been a wonderful idea if it hadn't been for the insects. I'd doze and then awake to the droning of mosquitos. After feeling several sizeable bites swelling on my cheekbone, and my lower lip hurting and ballooning, I admitted defeat and dragged back to my room.

I lit the lamp and moved to the mirror. The bites were worse than I'd feared. They were lumpy and red, and my mouth looked as if I'd been hit hard.

* * * * *

At first light I was up. After another difficult night I'd hit upon a way out of all this—an honorable, incredibly simple way to go home. The idea had been drumming around in my head since Jonas had first accused me of it. I'd get myself good and sick—I was halfway there already. I'd stop eating and work until I dropped in the dust. They'd have to see that though I'd done my best and hadn't uttered a word of complaint, this kind of life was no good for me. They'd send me home—not in disgrace, but with everyone's heartfelt concern. And Papa would take me back. If my health were broken, he would.

Before going down to the kitchen I donned the biggest dress I had, a drab brown muslin that hung on me like a sack. It helped—I looked thinner than ever. I powdered down my complexion until my newer tan color was gone and smudged some blacking beneath my eyes and into my cheeks to create a hollow effect. I looked ghastly. I put my hair in a rumpled bun and let the sides fall messily about my face. It did occur to me that I was overdoing it a trifle. The

64

change might be too shocking, but then who noticed me at all these days? It was just good for my vanity that Miles Lassiter wasn't around.

It was still too early to go down to the kitchen, but I went and began scrubbing walls. It was hard work and I longed to go back to bed, but I'd only toss in the heat as I'd done the night long.

"Well, well, cousin." Charity looked hard at me when later she burst through the door. "It's good to see you up and crackin'. Those walls are overdue for a scrub."

"Morning, Charity." I paused and moved closer to the windows so that she might better see my carefully coaxed pallor.

She turned and then stopped, her eyes fixing again upon mine. "Oh, Alex is feeling poorly again, so you'll have to do his chores today. The children can help like last time. That's a new dress, isn't it?"

I shook my head.

She shrugged. "Well, I'm off. I'm taking a ham to Misha—"

"Misha?" I couldn't believe she hadn't noticed my altered appearance.

"Papa's first wife. Oh, come on, Delores. You haven't forgotten Misha!"

Again I shook my head. No, I hadn't forgotten. That Clarey had been second wife to a man too poor to have one wife was something my family had never overlooked a minute.

"Hal says she's been running a fever lately, not sleeping at night. I might have to stay awhile and help."

That was it. She left. With all her talk of fevers and sleeplessness, why hadn't she noticed? And what was that remark about a new dress? This old thing couldn't look worse on me.

"Well, you're at it early, aren't you?" Jonas came in as I started the second wall. I felt him behind me staring down at my bent head. "Seems to me you ought to wait until it lightens up in here. You could do a more even job then."

Offended, I raised up. "Mr. Luker, thanks for the brilliant suggestion, but if I wait around I shan't have the opportunity of getting back to these walls. Today I not only have my own work to do but Alex Wubbleton's as well, and despite what you all seem to think, that gentleman does a great deal around here! We never seem to run out of work."

His smile was humorless. "At least *you* don't. You've become real dedicated, haven't you."

His sarcasm cut, and I found myself rubbing at my forehead. *Why did he have such a low opinion of me?* My head was hurting suddenly, and all the weariness of the past sleepless nights seemed to weigh down upon me. "If I said yes, Mr. Luker, you wouldn't believe it anyway. Think what you like."

He made no answer for a long while. I went back to my work. "You look ill, Lady D. Are you?"

It was my chance to try for his pity. I tried to think what I should say and opted for the truth. "I haven't been sleeping at night."

"Why not? With the hours you've been putting in, that's one thing that should come pretty easy."

"It's this awful heat. It makes me miserable."

The corner of his mouth lifted. "I can't change the weather for you, girl, but as long as you sprinkle down your sheets, you should be comfortable enough to sleep."

"Sprinkle my sheets?" The idea was ingenious. "With water?" Why hadn't I thought of that?

"Yeah. Just dampen down your sheets good, and they'll keep you cool. Didn't Charity show you that your first night here?"

"I—I suppose she didn't think of it." Or maybe she'd purposely forgotten to tell me. But I was ashamed at the thought. No one could be that mean. If I'd mentioned my discomfort to her—to anyone—I would have been told. It had been my pride. I'd suffered with the attitude of a martyr, and there'd been no need for it.

Thinking of the sleep I was sure to get later that night, I smiled with relief. "Thank you, Jonas, I'll do that. I'm sure it will help immensely."

He nodded and stepped away, but as he did so his head swung back around. "What have you got all over your face?"

Mortified, I shrank back into the shadows. Jonas would see what I'd done—understand my real motives. What a fool I was to even attempt such a thing. He saw through me with frightening accuracy: I would be found out, and the disgrace would be intolerable. Why hadn't I considered that? Exhaustion had driven me to this.

"Dust . . . dust. It's all over the place—flying in my eyes and mouth. Excuse me, but I've got to get back to work." Praying that he would revert to his normal disinterest and saunter on out, I wrung out my cloth and took a fierce swipe at the doorjam. I wasn't going through with it, of course. It had been a half-baked idea, hatched out of my irrational misery over not sleeping. As soon as I was alone, I'd scrub my face and redo my hair, and this time I'd try to remember that deceit never got me anywhere except into trouble. But Jonas wasn't going. He stood behind me, his eyes watchful. I could feel it. With another downward motion, my hand caught, and I gasped as a protruding sliver tore into my palm.

"A nail?" he asked as I hugged the stinging hand against me. "Let me see it."

"Just go and do whatever it is you need to do. It's only a sliver." Ignoring the injury I went on with my work, but still Jonas wouldn't leave.

"You're up to something, aren't you?" He spoke his words thoughtfully. "I've never seen you look more grim."

"It's just because I haven't been sleeping, but now that I

67

know what to do, I shall." I pushed the rag once more into the water, but too forcefully, for the suds splashed up and over my knees.

"Am I making you nervous, Lady D?"

"Would you please let me do my work in peace?"

"What is that white on your face? It's not dust." He took my arm and pulled me to my feet. "You haven't had your head in the flour bin, have you? It's powder, isn't it?"

His brows lowered as he looked at me. Obviously, there was little sense in shamming. "Yes, it's powder."

"Why?" But he knew the answer. It was there in his eyes. He could see it had been my purpose to look wretched, worked to exhaustion, and he would report my wickedness to Papa, he or Charity would. "Why, Lady?"

I could only hedge. "Why do you think a woman puts powder on her face?"

"You tell me, girl." The blue eyes had gone gray and steely. "And what have you done to your lip and cheek? Are those lumps more makeup?"

The bites! I shook out of his hold. "If you must know, I was bitten badly last night. I tried sleeping outside, you see, because of the heat, and the mosquitos were dreadful. I tried powdering them down so they wouldn't be so noticeable."

He didn't know whether or not to believe me. "But you've got powder everywhere—not just on the bites."

I laughed, tossing my head. "Of course. A woman must have even coloring."

"Lady, you're a bad liar, but you keep on trying, don't you? If you're trying something devious, hoping to find a way out of here, your Papa—"

68   "What a thing to say. How dare you!"

"You've always had your way! It must be quite a blow to find yourself locked in a situation where you are actually forced to play by the rules."

"I don't know what you're talking about."

"Then it's time you learn. Straighten up, Miss. We expect you to work but not to kill yourself in the process. When you've got a problem I want to know about it. Like this not sleeping—you should have said something before. If you keep up your little game, you'll be sorry you did."

A light leapt into his eyes as he spoke the threat, and I shivered. His face had hardened, his skin stretched taut over the ridges of his dark cheekbones. Mrs. Sackett's words knelled again in my brain, *"Wild blood, wild blood."*

"Don't you threaten me, Jonas Luker. I've been overworked here, but I've kept my mouth shut because you and Charity have just been waiting for me to complain. Oh, yes you have! You *want* me gone—*both* of you. Well, I haven't been willing to give you reason. I've done the work I've been assigned, and you've no reason, none, to be hounding me now."

I couldn't face him a minute longer. I bolted for the bathroom and locked the door behind me. Not until my face was scrubbed clean and my hair done to perfection did I dare go back to finish the walls.

SIX

The sky was smudged and dark in the south, and I thought this was a sign of rain. If I had been looking closer, I might have seen otherwise, but Old Dog was whining behind me and yapping as if he wanted to go back already, and it was so hot. The heat lay like a blanket against my skin, a woolly, prickly warmth that made me itch with the awfulness of it. And so when I saw the strange smear on the horizon, I felt an elation. Rain was coming—wet, wonderful rain and with it, cool, drenched-clean air. Just the thought made breathing easier, and I opened my mouth with a long, satisfying sigh.

I hadn't appreciated rain properly before, but after these long, dry weeks, I knew I would never take rain for granted again. So maybe I had learned one lesson, and Papa, if he knew, would be glad.

"Old Dog!" I called to hurry the mangy creature and quickened my pace. Already the wind was starting, and it wouldn't do to be caught midway in a downpour. No, if the rain hit before I got there, I'd have to turn around and walk back to the inn without my visit to Debra. I couldn't very well go knocking at their door soaked to the skin.

I began to run, holding my skirts out of the flying dust.

70

"Old Dog, Old Dog—" I turned in the whirling dust and squinted after the squirrelly beast, but he was gone—off chasing lizards or grasshoppers no doubt. If he couldn't keep to my heels like a suitable pet, then he would get left behind.

My eyes began to hurt from straining out dust, and the air was growing thick with it. The wind whipped it against my face in a stinging onslaught. I sought the approaching cloud for the rain I had so much anticipated, but my parched lids snapped closed on a horrifying sight. No moisture was hidden in that reddish murk. It closed down upon me and the land with a hot, suffocating hand. Dust storm! Papa had told a wild tale about dust storms . . .

The truth of my situation had no sooner dawned on me than it became impossible to see. The sand was denser than fog and more frightening because with every breath I took a mouthful. I stumbled onward in the blindness with my head and back bowed knowing full well I could be hopelessly lost by such a course, but I was driven by the morbid vision of being buried alive.

"Papa!" I wasn't really crying, but I was scared and alone and couldn't think what I could do that wouldn't put me in even greater jeopardy. "Why did you send me to such a place? Was I such a bad daughter?"

I turned back in what I thought was the direction I had come, but there was no telling now. I tripped again and again, the ground full of pot holes. When finally I went down against a clump of chaparral, I stayed put, pulling my skirt about my head, trying hard not to think about the grisly account of the baron buried in the Mojave with nothing showing but a withering hand. I curled into a ball with my face in my lap and my knees pressed against the scorched desert floor. Stupid girl!

Only an hour before, Charity had warned that the weather hadn't felt right, that I ought to postpone my visit, and Old Dog had complained the entire way, nipping at my

71

dress and then deserting altogether. Stupid girl, always so sure of everything and listening to nothing and nobody! "You've got to learn." Papa's words droned over and over in my head until they seemed one with the caterwauling voice of the wind. "How many times must I tell you, Delores, you've got to learn?"

"Learn what, Papa? What is it I do that makes you so angry?"

He'd thrown up his hands at that and left the room.

"You're so popular, Delores Lyn—accepted in all the right circles. It makes me so proud, and your mother would be too if she were here." Grandmother Rachael had made me believe it with my whole heart, and none of it had been true! Immediately after her death I'd been hit by a tidal wave of denouncement. If my behavior had been so unbearable, why hadn't anyone said so? Why?

I began to feel the weight of the sand against me, pressing me down. I could scarcely lift my head. I began to sob.

The howling vanished as quickly as it had come. I lay beneath my makeshift shroud and listened to the hush. Sure that the nightmare had played itself out, I threw off my skirt and looked at the sand blown smooth about me. I wasn't exactly sure where I was, but I knew my direction. I shook out my clothing, lifted my chin, and began back toward town. I was still sobbing, which made no sense and which was totally unlike me. But it was just that I suddenly had too many enemies to handle—the upbringing I'd trusted and clung to, the people about me, and this horrid place with its infernal heat and sudden storms.

I turned to see a rider coming from out of nowhere.

72   "This does it. This really does it!" Jonas swore, and I wanted to run. "Charity told you not to go and yet you did—straight into the dust storm without a thought for anyone—not yourself—or for those who'd be sent out to find you."

He yanked the neckerchief further off his face, but his hardening jaw gave me little reassurance. "Lady Delores, I'm going to give you the tanning of your life, and if you ever . . ." He swung down off the horse and finished his threat with a swift lunge toward me. I ducked under his arm and fell with a thump on the ground.

"Don't you touch me, you filthy savage!" It was the first time I'd referred to his ancestry, and I knew I'd said the wrong thing. I stared a moment at his clenched jaw, then scrambled to my feet and tried to run, but his hand caught my elbow and held me fast. "Let me go, Jonas Luker, you—" I bit off *barbarian* and tried to think of some insulting label that wouldn't hit at his forebears. After all, I was an educated woman. Prejudice (when one felt it) shouldn't show. "You . . . you uncivilized brute!" I finished, then winced as he flung me full force over his knee. "You can't, Jonas. You've got to be kidding!" I shrieked upside down, horrified at his brutish treatment of me. I had never been spanked in my life. Never! And when the flying blow hit my backside, even all my petticoats did not soften the pain. It shot through me with shuddering force. Then I was turned up and set hard upon my feet.

"Maybe now you will have learned." He ground out the words. There it was again—that vague reference to my nebulous shortcomings.

"Learned what, Jonas Luker? Why is everyone always hammering at me to learn—Papa, Debra, Mary, Charity, and now you! What is so wrong with me anyway? I didn't plan that storm. And Charity did not tell me to stay home. She only said the weather didn't *feel* right. I've been here for weeks, and the only thing I've seen is the inside of that inn." I struggled to repin my straggly hair, but it was no use. "Without my walks to Debra's, I'd go mad—*mad, do you hear me?*"

His hand came toward me, and I shot out of reach. "Let me be! If you ever touch me again, Mr. Luker, I'll shoot you through and through. And that's no idle threat either. I do have a gun—it's Papa's and I'll use it."

The injury that had just been delivered to my person was of no account; but my pride was shattered, and the tears I'd always kept on such a tight rein fell without restraint. So what if Jonas Luker saw? I had little more to lose. He'd become an enemy to rival the silent sun, and from this moment on I would never forget it.

"Get on!" He'd mounted his horse and had ridden abreast of me, holding out a long, brown arm. "Delores, *get on!*"

I sidestepped him and changed direction. "Careful, Lady—" He turned the horse and glowered at me from his saddle. "I'd hate to have to repeat that little lesson—"

I wasn't thinking or perhaps I wouldn't have done it, but something went *snap* inside me. I knelt and my hands fastened about a stone. I didn't really aim, but the rock hit the horse's rump, and it reared back and shot ahead in a full gallop. I nearly laughed at Jonas's stunned expression, but the humor was quickly snuffed when Jonas, caught off balance, fell. Hoofs flashed briefly near his head, then the horse was gone, and Jonas was still as death on the ground.

I tore across the distance and flung myself down at his side.

"You fool girl!"

I was just inches from his face, and I straightened. "Are you all right?"

"Yes, and it's a good thing, too!"

"You deserved it, Mr. Luker." I was unrepentant—at least outwardly. Within I felt an almost singing gratitude that I hadn't hurt him. "You can't treat me like that and get away with it."

"Maybe not—" It was a small concession, but it made me feel mountains better.

"I'm sorry you came looking for me, but I was fine."

"You looked fine—walking toward Kanab with your hair shot full of sand and crying your eyes out."

"I wasn't really crying, and I was walking in the direction of town. I'm good at directions."

"You're lousy at them. St. George is over there."

I finally accepted the ride back into town—not because I'd forgiven Jonas Luker, but because in small part I'd evened the score. I'd nearly killed the man, and he did have the devil of a time coaxing his horse back.

SEVEN

"Lady D?" Jonas called to me the next day. "You've got a caller."

I wiped my hands and looked in the mirror I'd mounted inside one of the cupboard doors. At least Debra wouldn't find me quite the haggard mess I'd been on her last visit. My hair was done up with curls framing my face, I was wearing a frilly white blouse and gray skirt, and I'd even taken the trouble of applying makeup that morning, though with my heated complexion it was scarcely necessary. I took off my apron and smoothed my blouse down.

"Debra?" I called as I walked into the parlor. But it wasn't Debra. It was Connan Trouseman, the one who'd behaved so brutishly the night of my abduction. He was scrubbed and wore a clean shirt, and his wet hair was plastered to one side of his head.

I felt my smile fade. "Mr. Trouseman, are you waiting to see me?"

"Yes, ma'am, and you can call me Connan—or Con, if you prefer."

I smiled fleetingly at that. "I prefer Mr. Trouseman, thank you."

He looked at me and then away, plucking at his shirt

front. "Have you seen that purple dress yet—the one your sister picked out for ya? It'll replace the one we spoilt."

I nodded. "We?"

"Me and the guys. I want to make sure you're not holdin' bad feelin's agin us."

"The dress makes up for the other one."

He rubbed his hands together. "Good, good. I talked with yer sister, and she thought it'd be all right if I was to take you to the dance next week."

"I'm sorry, but that isn't possible." I saw no reason not to come straight out with a refusal. This man had to know that I could *never* entertain feelings for him.

"Well, why not?" He seemed actually stunned. "Mrs. Stubbs says you haven't met anyone yet, and—"

"But I have. Thank you, anyway." I took a step toward the door. "Now if you'll excuse me, I'm working—"

"Hold on there." He scowled down at the hat he was holding. "I'll go when ya tell me who it is takin' you."

I blinked at his sudden rudeness. "*Pardon?*"

"Who is it takin' you? Not one of my group—they all know I've spoke for ya. So who is it?"

"I—I—" I stammered about, off guard at his obstinacy. "You'll see at the dance, won't you? But then, maybe we won't be going at all. It's up to him."

Mr. Trouseman swore at that. "Ya haven't been asked. I know it. Yer jes' makin' excuses so's not to go with me. But I'm first in line, and ya can't accept no other invitations."

"I've told you—"

"You've told me nuthin'!" He pushed a hand across his slack mouth. "Gimme a name, or I'll not leave."

My first thought was Miles Lassiter. He'd surely do me the favor of escorting me to the dance, but I hadn't seen him in weeks, and it could be weeks more before he returned. "I'm going with Jonas Luker."

Fabrication—deceit, *again*. "Jonas has a lot going on right now," I backpedaled, "so our plans *may* change. But really, Mr. Trouseman, I don't have any need to explain to you."

"Hah, I don't believe it about Jonas." But he did believe me. Already he'd withdrawn his repulsively familiar manner, and that loathsome gleam in his eye was gone. "He likes Melissa Stubbs—has fer years. If he's takin' anyone, it'll be her."

"I'll call him in, and you can ask him then." I stepped to the entry. "Jonas? Jonas? Mr. Trouseman would like to speak with you a minute, please."

I held my breath for fear Jonas might really appear, but there was no need. The obnoxious Connan Trouseman was already leaving, stomping down the porch steps like an angry bull.

* * * * *

The dance was Friday evening, but not until late Monday afternoon was I able to have a private word with Jonas. He was in the office he shared with Charity, and books and papers were stacked indiscriminately everywhere. "It's a mess," he admitted without apology, then turned back to the ledger in front of him.

"I have a problem, Mr. Luker—it has to do with Connan Trouseman."

He nodded, not looking up.

"You know he came to see me Saturday—"

"Yes, and the day before that too," he put in absently.

"Oh? No one told me about his other visit."

"That's because I sent him packing. He'd been drinking. Why don't you sit down? Don't let a little clutter stop you."

"I'm fine standing."

At last he glanced at me. "You don't look it. What's the matter?"

"Nothing—I mean, well, I'm trying to tell you." His gaze was puzzled, but even so he shifted back to the desk to alter a figure. *"Would you put that down a moment!"* I hadn't meant to say that, so I added more contritely, "Forgive me for interrupting you, but this is quite urgent, and I'll hurry with it."

He let the book close and pushed back in his chair. "I'm listening."

"Mr. Trouseman has asked me to the dance this week—naturally, I've told him no."

"So?"

"He has a hard time accepting that. He demanded to know who I—"

"Let him demand all he wants. Con has a temper, but it won't do him any good if you ignore him."

"I wish it were that simple. The man scares me."

Jonas's lips twitched into a smile of disbelief. "I've seen you handle Con and half a dozen others equally as rough. You can take care of yourself, Lady. You're a dragon slayer if ever there was one."

"A dragon slayer?" I was offended and didn't bother to hide it. The conversation had taken a difficult turn. How was I to maneuver him into asking me to the dance if he didn't feel I needed protecting? "If you remember right, I was nearly burned alive at the shivaree party, and if you hadn't been there, I don't know what might have happened to me."

"What's this?" His eyes widened in mockery. "A belated thank-you?"

"I—well, I guess it is. I do thank you for protecting me the way you did." My cheeks flamed with embarrassment, but it had to be done. "And what I'm asking now is—"

"Yes, what *are* you asking now?"

"I, well, I need your protection again."

He looked behind him at the blank wall. "From what? I don't see anything."

"I've already *told* you—from Mr. Trouseman."

His smile broadened, and he shook his head at me. "I

79

know Con Trouseman is rather a poor excuse for a man, but he's nothing to be afraid of. Some silly girl might even find him to be the man of her dreams." He was laughing at me.

It was almost impossible to keep my tone civil. "Tell me, please, are you going to the dance this week?"

He lifted his shoulders and, after a momentary lapse, drawled, "If Melissa Stubbs accepts when I ask *her*, then yes. Why? Would you like me to keep an eye on Con and see he behaves with you?"

"Would you listen?" My hand flew outward in a gesture of frustration and hit the paper file, spilling the sheaves across the floor at my feet. "Con Trouseman is not going to be with me! How many times must I tell you that?"

Jonas's eyes narrowed at my burst of temper, then simultaneously we stooped to retrieve the papers. I couldn't believe he could be so obtuse. It had to be deliberate. I could see in his eyes that he *knew* what I wanted of him.

"Oh? Are you going alone, or—"

"I had hoped, Mr. Luker, I had hoped someone *else* might ask me. That would make my refusal of Con more definite, you see?" His head was next to mine and, taking advantage of our closeness, I gave him a pleading look, eyes wide, lips parted. It was one of my best expressions. I knew because Egan had told me when I implored him in that manner he could never say no. But obviously with Jonas Luker it was no good. He was already turning away, shifting back into his seat.

"Well, I wouldn't hold my breath if I were you, Lady."

"You wouldn't?" I asked stupidly, stunned at his blunt refusal.

"Nope." His mouth flattened into a grim smile (of distaste, I thought). "The guys I know realize how foolish it would be to start dating you."

He was speaking of himself. He wouldn't take me— worse, was repulsed by me, and he took no care to even hide it. "I—I don't understand, Jonas. I don't understand," I stammered. Never had a man been so cruel as to reject me so utterly, and to my face! His words had cut me to the quick. I battled to retrieve my poise, but it was further from reach than it had ever been. Tears threatened to burst through, and I had no choice but to keep silent, or the dam would break and humiliate me even more.

The whimpering of Old Dog scratching at the kitchen door filled the painful silence, and the big clock in the entry began to chime four. Meg would be fixing supper. I had to somehow walk out the door.

"Wait a minute, Lori—" Using my childhood name instead of his usual derisive *Lady D* was the worst thing he could have done right then. "I think you misunderstood me. When I said it would be foolish to date you—"

"No, no!" I smiled through stiff, trembling lips. "I'm sure I understood *perfectly* well. But you needn't worry, Mr. Luker, I'm only momentarily . . . momentarily . . ."

I was unable to finish, for my eyes were filling.

He was leaving his chair now and moving to the doorway. "Lori, as your employer it would be foolish to—"

"That isn't what you meant at all, and you know it! You're just trying to do a quick patch job."

"You're still getting the wrong idea here. I'm sorry I—"

"Don't be! I was simply trying to prove to that oaf Trouseman that I was unavailable. I was willing to ask anybody to take me to the stupid dance—anybody, do you hear? But you're right. I'm a dragon slayer of the first order. I can handle Con Trouseman or anyone else just fine on my own—without your help!"

Somehow I managed to scramble past him and duck into the kitchen, my face still dry and my head held high.   81

EIGHT

"It's been a delight spending the morning with you," Clarey said, as she looked up from her needlework. "But you ought to get out now before it gets too hot and enjoy a little of your free day. Why don't you ask Jonas to hitch up the buggy for you and take a ride out to see Debra?"

I sighed and closed the book in my lap.

"You seem depressed today. That isn't like you, dear. What's the matter?"

"I don't know."

"You're probably a little homesick. You've been here—what, six weeks? And you're hardly ever out of the kitchen. You don't have to work quite so hard, you know. Charity's very happy with your work. You've surprised her with your diligence."

"Have I? She hasn't said as much to me."

"I'm afraid that since this thing with her husband, Charity is rather uncommunicative. She's probably a mite resentful of you, too."

"Why? What have I done?"

"It isn't what you've done, but what you are. You're young, unmarried, free. All your major choices are still ahead of you while Charity's are in the past. Randall has disappointed her, taken her dignity, and left her to shoulder his responsibility and his humiliation alone. She's in a situation she can't get out of."

"She could divorce the man. He's in prison. Surely the Church authorities would understand."

"Maybe. But it's more complex than that. She loves him, and there are the children."

"She loves him—after all he's done, she still loves him?" Nothing I'd seen or heard since my arrival had prepared me for that. Charity couldn't love Randall Raines. His name was *never* mentioned in her presence.

"Oh, yes, dear, *she does.* They had some very good years together, and that makes it all the harder, don't you know."

"If a man did that to me, I'd leave him in a minute."

Clarey laughed. "Other people's problems seem so simple to solve, don't they? Randall was a good and fine man in many ways, and Charity recalls how it was before he took the money. It's a tragic thing to fall in love with the wrong man. Tragic! Don't *you* fall for the wrong man, Delores. Take your time and be sure of yourself before you marry anybody."

"Dearest Clarey." I couldn't help smiling. "Of course I shan't marry the wrong man. I shall only marry someone who can take me to the temple. He must be respectable, rich, and good!"

"And wasn't Egan Stone all those things?"

"Grandma!" Aldan, red-faced and tearful, burst through the door and stood before the bed whining. "Grandma, Mara's doing it again. She won't let me be teacher!"

"My, my, why can't you two get along? Delores, would you go settle this? I'm tired and could sleep a little before lunch."

I left with Aldan's grubby little hand in my own. Mara, a mere ten minutes older than her brother, was forever assuming a position over him. Her spunk was both mildly endearing and obnoxious. She loved to instruct and was constantly doing it—even to me.

"You do know why people are called *human beans,* don't you, Lori?" she had asked me once on an evening walk.

"Human beans?" I hid a smile.

"Yes, know why?"

"No, I can't say I do."

"So as to not mix us up with all the other kinds." Her tone was triumphant.

"Of beans, you mean?"

"That's right. If we were all just called beans, then how would we even know what we're talking about?"

"You have an amazing power to reason, Mara," I'd complimented her and been rewarded with a dimpled smile.

"Tattletale!" she screeched now as I entered the playroom at Aldan's side. "Don't you know only babies run and tell?"

"Mara, what are you talking about? Aldan and I are on our way to Hobb's for a sweet, and we thought you might like to come along. Perhaps we were wrong. You seem to be in a terrible mood, and as it's my free day I can't have you hanging about me with a long face."

She somehow managed to transform her visage into one of angelic radiance. "Oh, please, Lori, I'll be so good. I'm through being teacher. Anyway, it's Aldan's turn. We'll all go get the sweets, and then we can come back, and I'll be the pupil for an hour."

Aldan was delighted with that, and we left to walk in the sunshine beneath the trees that grew along the grassy canal banks. I was amazed at my prowess in handling children. (With Egan's, I'd been a complete failure.) Despite my low mood, the presence of the children lifted me, and before long we were laughing together and singing the sorry song of the cottonwood farmer who was called to Dixie.

84

* * * * *

It was well after two when I started for Debra's. I walked to avoid having to ask Jonas for the buggy. I'd dressed in a short-sleeved green eyelet dress with a wide-brimmed, ribboned hat so the heat wasn't as bad as it might have been. I was getting to know a few of the faces from church, and I waved and nodded to those who waved at me, grateful for anyone's kindness to me these days.

I'd left the shade of the trees behind me for quite a distance when a buggy going in the same direction slowed and then stopped. A man called a friendly hello, but this time I didn't respond.

"Hey, beautiful, want a ride?"

I cast him a quick, cool look. He was young, probably younger than I, sandy haired and clean cut.

"I'm Skeeter, remember?"

I didn't, so I hurried on.

"Delores, don't you remember me? I'm a friend of Debra's and Mel's. Skeeter Austin. You were out there last week. I was helping with the house."

"Oh!" I blushed, feeling silly for being afraid. This was the young man who was so enamored with Mel's sister, Melissa. He was so often hanging about on the flimsiest of excuses that Mel had finally given him a job on the house.

"It's a hot day for walkin'. I'll give you a lift if you like."

"You're most generous to stop." I accepted his hand up into the battered buggy. It was old and creaked over the uneven ground, but it was refreshing riding. The breeze made by the loping horse was cooling, and I sat back against the patched upholstery and listened to Skeeter talk about the progress on Debra's home. It wasn't until we'd arrived and he was helping me out that a thought occurred to me.

"Skeeter, who are you taking to the dance Friday?"

"No one. There's only one girl I'd wanna ask, and she's going with someone else."

"Who's that?"

He gave me a worried frown—reluctant to answer me. "Melissa—she's going with Jonas."

"But she isn't, Skeeter. Jonas hasn't asked her yet."

"Don't matter. He will."

"Not necessarily." Some inner spite made me add, "It's

very late—what if he *doesn't* ask? Melissa is sure to be crushed, left high and dry without a date."

"She wouldn't go with me. She—"

"But she will! She likes you. I saw how she was when I was here." From what everyone had said about her, I knew Melissa was "nice." She was the kind of girl who would accept the *first* invitation received. "And you've nothing to lose and everything to gain by trying, haven't you, Skeeter?"

His boyish mouth worked in thought. "Yeah. I guess I could *try*."

He walked up to the door of the old farmhouse, knocked, and since it was Melissa who answered and invited us in, I was privileged to witness the invitation and her hesitant acceptance of it.

Skeeter thanked her with the humbleness of a schoolboy and bounded out of the house, but not before giving me a wide smile of gratitude. Thanks to me, Melissa Stubbs would be on *his* arm Friday night and not Jonas Luker's!

* * * * *

"Isn't *what* odd?" I asked Debra as I pulled off my shoes, wishing I could do the same with my stockings. It was so awfully warm. We were out behind the Stubbses' house under two huge trees that kept the sun off. The scrub lawn was more a flat weed than anything else, but I was relieved to be away from that sugary sweet Melissa, who, despite what happened to her, kept that insipid smile.

"Jonas Luker hasn't been by to ask Melissa to the dance," Debra answered. "She's been counting on that for days now. It seems he's stopped coming here at all. I don't think she even *sees* him anymore except at church, and then he does nothing more than sit with her."

"I don't think it's odd. Obviously Jonas doesn't care for her as much as she thought he did."

"The way everybody talks, it's almost as if they were engaged. And another thing—Skeeter Austin is afraid of his shadow, and yet he mustered up the courage to ask Melissa out."

"Oh, Debra, how much courage does it take to ask a girl for a simple date?"

"A lot, when it's Jonas Luker's girl you're asking."

Debra looked at me long and hard, then asked in an undertone, "You're not behind it, are you, Lori?"

Not wanting to hear the question, I didn't, but sighed and pushed to my feet. "You know, one has to admit this country has a certain beauty—so wild and untamed. If it weren't for all the inconveniences here, the heat and dreariness—" I turned to see Debra glaring at me.

"You can't do it, Lori! You just can't! Jonas Luker is terribly attractive, I admit, but he doesn't mean anything to you. But he's everything to Melissa. She loves him, and he loves her!"

"So if he loves her, then why doesn't he come by anymore?" I felt no guilt at all, for while I might have ruined his chances of taking Melissa to the dance, I couldn't be blamed for Jonas's sudden absences here. And he'd made no bones about not caring for me or my looks. *Terribly attractive*, Debra had said of him. Well, not to me he wasn't.

"Are you making some sort of play for him?"

I laughed at that. "Oh, Deb, you flatter me, but honestly, Jonas Luker is safe from me, and your Melissa can rest assured. I'm not so bored here that I have to amuse myself with the likes of Jonas Luker. I'm finding it almost enjoyable to work hard—look at my hands. Grandmother would be mortified."

"Yes, but Papa would be proud. I've written him telling him how ill you looked on my first visit to the inn. He was concerned."

87

"Honestly?" I ignored a sudden twinge of hurt. Papa hadn't written me in all this time—not once.

"Yes. He said you should be broken into such physical labor more gradually and that I should go and talk to Clarey."

"It isn't necessary, thanks."

"Maybe not, but you still seem worn out, and you're much too thin. Papa wants to know if you're happy here."

"And what did you tell him?"

"The truth—that you're miserable and you can't be forced to stay too long or it will ruin your health."

"Oh, Debra—it would be much more politic to tell him I'm having the time of my life. Don't you see he wants me to be miserable? If you tell him I'm happy, he'll see the futility of this and have me back. Write and tell him you were mistaken—say that I'm delirious with dates and attention and that I'm loving every minute of it."

"I suppose that's what you've been writing?" she asked.

"Of course. I've been very creative, telling him about the warm, sun-filled days, the color in my cheeks, that Charity and I are as close as sisters, how friendly I'm finding everyone, how rugged and romantic are the men—"

"But that isn't how you feel!"

"It's how I shall feel given some time. I can't go about with my chin dragging or things never will get better for me."

"I like that about you, Lori. You really are indomitable."

"Thank you, Deb. So are you!"

"Not like you!" She laughed, then switched to a subject I hadn't dared broach. "Guess what! Papa's forgiven me for marrying Mel."

"Already?" I wasn't sure I believed her, but then Papa was so fond of Debra.

"You know that Papa never gets angry with *me*." She grinned with self-importance, unwittingly pointing out the difference in Papa's attitude toward the two of us. "Oh, he's disappointed, but at least he's accepted that I'm grown and able to do as I choose." She hesitated a moment, and then said, "I haven't told him that Mel isn't a churchgoer. He's asked when we're to be sealed, and I told him that we'll get it taken care of as soon as possible. You won't mention in your letters that Mel is inactive, will you? I just know he'll come around in time—when he sees what the gospel can do for our life together. Papa won't ever have to know about that part of it."

I hoped for Debra's sake it would work out that way. "I'll not say a word, but you might mention this to Clarey. She's worried, too."

Debra froze. "Oh, my! What if I'm too late? I'll drive you back right now and talk to her."

As it turned out, Cousin Clarey had written to Papa several times, "but no, I haven't mentioned Mel's church standing. I've tried to concentrate more on the positive side to your husband."

"Oh, thank you, Clarey. Mel is a dear and sensitive man, and he's already half-promised to attend sacrament meeting with me soon."

Clarey's smile was indulgent. "I'll believe it, Debra Sue, when I see it. You work hard on Mel, and I'll keep quiet, but if your father should ask outright about Mel's religious views, I shall have no choice but to answer honestly."

It was all Debra could ask for, and after she wished Clarey a good day, I walked Debra back to her horse and the little, canopied, yellow-wheeled cart Mel had recently surprised her with. "It's been a lovely day, Deb. Thanks. See you Sunday."

"Not Friday? You're definitely not going to the dance then?"

"Maybe next time. Meg says there's always another one coming up."

"If you're sure."

She grinned and shook the reins over the black pony. The cart lurched about, tearing down the road, dust flying. I watched until Debra disappeared, smiling at the comical way her hair flew out behind her, matching the pony's flaring mane and tail. She seemed so young to be married.

NINE

"So it's ugly, is it? 'A barbaric, ugly, uncivilized place'?" Mr. Wubbleton shook his white head and laughed—an unusually young laugh, his grainy voice echoing in the dimming streets.

"Yes, it is. *It is!*" He wanted me to take back the words I'd spoken in frustration on my first walk with him, but I couldn't. "Tell me, sir, if your wife and daughter have been dead so many years, why have you stayed? It doesn't make any sense."

"It was too late to leave. Dixie had already cast its spell on me." He leaned hard on his cane. "You'll see what I mean, I promise you. You keep telling yourself you're not fond of St. George, little one, but already it's getting its grip on you. When you leave us to return home to the green valley you talk so much about, you'll never forget the way it was here, and with the memory there will always be a longing to return—to stand here and smell the desert, and see the black hills cutting off the sun, to experience just once more the night coming down like this—"

"Oh, Mr. Wubbleton, the way you talk."

"Shhh, listen!" Someone was blowing a harmonica, and the melancholy whine became a concert with the night sounds about us: the crickets chirring in the grass of the canals, the hurrying wheels of a passing carriage, the breeze rustling like voices in the trees above us. All about us lay the land I hated—the silent, dead, treeless hills that boxed in the heat and held me so far from home and Papa. But perhaps I didn't really hate Dixie but was blaming it for what was at fault in me. If there was beauty here it went well with loneliness, and now as the brilliant colors faded with shadows, I did draw a kind of peace from the watching hills, as I had done from those of such a different hue at home.

"The mountains guard you, rest from care . . . good-night . . ." I murmured a line from a half-remembered lullaby my mother had sung to me as a child.

"I beg your pardon, my dear?"

"Oh, it's nothing, Alex—just part of an old song. May I call you Alex, please?"

"Of course, of course!" His withered hand covered mine on his elbow. "Though why you refuse to fall in with the rest and call me *Wubbles* is beyond me. I truly don't mind. It's fond, and friendly."

"It doesn't carry the respect you deserve, Alex. I admire you tremendously."

"I thank you for that." His tone wavered, and I knew he was thinking of the horrible incident that had occurred less than an hour ago with Charity. Old Dog had romped through Charity's laundry, dragging and spilling her newly washed clothes about the garden. Then, to top it off, after dinner I'd been caught feeding the creature, and Charity had hit the ceiling. I couldn't resist berating her.

"You really are the limit, Cousin Charity! How can you deny the dog when he's so old and thin?"

"I will not feed every stray you romanticize over! That stupid dog is useless—a pest to me and our guests, a flea trap that never saw a useful day in his life."

"Mr. Wubbleton will hear you, Charity. Hush!"

"Don't you hush me! Let him hear. Let him! We've kept that lazy hound for no other reason than to placate old Wubbles—a guest that doesn't even pay! I've had it with the both of them—freeloaders!"

The creak of the kitchen door was enough to make her

pause in her tirade, and we turned together to see Alex peering out through the screen at us. "I'm sorry to trouble you, Miss Charity, for I know I've been a burden since my money ran out. But it may ease your mind to know I've written again to Mr. Neason concerning the sale of my Idaho land—"

"Oh, Wubbles!" Charity's hands flew to her head in exasperation. "How many times have I heard that? 'The money will be coming any day now for certain.' You mean well, but I have a hard time paying bills with good intentions."

"Charity, don't." I knew she would regret what she was saying, and I hated to see the defenseless old gentleman hurt.

She turned on me. "What do you know about it, high and mighty cousin, with your rich Papa and your trunks of dresses and lace? What have you ever wanted for in this life that you didn't immediately receive? Every month I promise Jonas and his brothers that we'll make a profit, and every month Jonas must sell off more of his cattle just to keep us going. Did you know his brothers have been pushing to have the house sold—and then what will we do? We who depend upon this roof? This is a business, and it comes down to this—we can't afford to keep what does not produce. And that list is getting heavy—my babies, my mother, Old Dog, Wubbles, and you, Delores, though I admit you are contributing, though it's scarcely enough to balance—"

"Enough!" It was Jonas, and his snarl brought Charity around in stunned silence.

"Jonas, tell them! I'm only one pers—"

"Go inside! I'll be in to finish this." And as she balked, "Do it, Charity! Now!"

92

Charity fled into the house, and Jonas clasped a hand on Alex's shoulder and spoke with a gentle sincerity that almost made me like him. "She doesn't mean it. You are family to us and are welcome and needed here. Randall's mother was here today. Charity's close to cracking or she'd never have said those things to you."

The old man nodded once and, not looking at either of us, shuffled off to sit behind the grape arbor.

"He's hurting," I said.

"Yes." Jonas raked the straight hair from his eyes. "And so is Charity, and Randall, and you, and the rest of mankind!" He strode back into the house, letting the screen door thunder shut behind him.

* * * * *

I hadn't been able to leave it alone. Alex had been hurt—Charity's words had torn the heart right out of him. Didn't she see what I saw—a man struggling to keep his pride? His careful way of dressing—the frayed jacket and shapeless pants, the starched yellowed shirts. Freeloader? Why, he was always tinkering about, fixing things, working in the garden, watering, visiting Clarey and boosting her spirits, helping with the children. He brought so much to us all. When it came down to it, he was my best friend here, he'd accepted me on sight, and I loved him.

"Mr. Wubbleton, forgive me, but are you all right?"

He turned and smiled at me, and the tears in his eyes brought tears to my own.

"Oh, Mr. Wubbleton, please don't think about it. Just wipe those lies out of your mind—"

"But it's true—I'm a used-up old man, Miss Ashley, and they've carried me long enough. It's hurtful to rely on others, and I've got to settle up somehow. I can't hold my head up until I do."

"But that land you've got. Surely Charity can wait until it's sold."

"No, I don't think she can. I don't know why I don't hear from them—" He lifted tired shoulders. "But don't you fret, Miss. You said at dinner you would be taking a walk—you'd better get at it or the light will be gone."

"Come with me. I don't want to go alone."

Without answering he'd pushed to his feet and we'd crossed the side lawn and turned down the street toward the temple . . .

93

Now it was dark. The walk had been good. As we climbed the steps of the brightly lit guesthouse, I knew Alex was feeling better, but the problem was still in both our minds. How could he pay his bill? The sum had to be sizable.

Maybe I should write Papa. He wouldn't like my asking for money outright—it would mean another black mark against me, but for Alex, I'd risk further disapproval.

TEN

"Well, I can't get Connan to go," Meg said. "I've told him you're busy, but, Delores, the man won't listen. He's waiting on the front porch with the kids. I don't like him with the children, do you?"

It was late Thursday afternoon, and the kitchen had become hotter than a boiler room. We'd moved to the outside kitchen in back of the inn, had taken a good portion of the afternoon cleaning out the seldom-used ovens and shifting pots and utensils, and with Alex's help, we'd propped up a makeshift table to work on until Jonas could construct something more solid.

The flies were miserable, and despite Alex's efforts, the chimney to one of the ovens remained blocked, and the fire and soot came back into our faces every time we had to turn the potatoes. All in all, it had been a trying day.

Jonas and Charity had been gone since early the day before. (He had had to go to Pine Valley, and Charity was visiting with friends in Washington.) Clarey had stubbornly insisted on leaving her bed to help Meg's girls clean, but her strength hadn't held, and in less than an hour she was forced back to her bed with her leg paining as it hadn't done in a long time.

Mara and Aldan, bored and cross with the heat themselves, had been constantly at my skirts asking for a bowl to lick, or just one more honey drop, please, and wouldn't I stop and come see what Aldan had caught in the pretty box? I was certainly not in the mood for another visit from Connan Trouseman.

Without removing my damp apron, and not bothering to even wash my face, I marched around the inn to the front porch and glared at the man, who was slouched idly in the chair swing, chewing noisily on a long stem of peppermint. Mara and Aldan were perched on the porch railing opposite with a sweets box between them, explaining about the rare and wonderful creature they had inside and about how important it was that enough holes were punched in the box so the thing could breathe and "not strangulate."

"What is it, Mr. Trouseman, that's so all-fired important?"

"Afternoon, Miss Delores, afternoon." He didn't bother getting to his feet, but shifted so his dirty boots scraped up the railing, leaving a trail of mud behind.

"Mara and Aldan, would you please run and see if Meggie needs some help?"

"But we haven't shown Mr. Trouseman what we caught—"

"Leave it and do it later, Aldan. Now mind, both of you." At the note of command in my voice, they slid down into the lilac beds, leaped the canal, and escaped into the neighbor's hedge. I turned back to Connan Trouseman.

He gave me a greenish grin. "Somethin' happened today. Mighty interesting."

"Mr. Trouseman, I'm sure I wouldn't find it interesting at all. Now, excuse me, please, but I've got work to do."

"Hey, wait up." He jumped the railing and caught me by the shoulders. "Don't go running off all the time. You're not the only one with a job. I've been helpin' out yer brother-in-law. Jonas was out there yesterday—and not to lend no hand neither."

"Mr. Trouseman—"

"He was there to ask his Missy to the dance tomorra.

Right there in front of the bunch of us, he sez, 'What time shall I pick you up Friday, Melissa honey?' Now isn't that strange—him asking her to the dance when you said he was goin' with you?"

"Obviously, Mr. Trouseman, I lied."

He laughed at that, a wheezing, wet sniggle that sprayed me revoltingly. "Ya did! Ya sure did—bold as ya please. Now I've been thinkin' about that. Why would ya lie outright—unless it's cuz yer skeered a ol' Con, ummm?"

"Mr. Trouseman, let me go this instant." I tried to move back out of his hold, but his hands slid from my shoulders to my arms, and he jerked me against him. "Ya don't need to be skeered, girlie. Jest make friends with me, and we could have a roarin' good time—"

"I won't go with you. Now let me go, please."

Refusing him had been the wrong thing to say. His hands dug into my arms. "If'n you'd feel easier-like, we could double up with Mel and yer sis."

I looked about for help from someone, but I didn't dare move a muscle. This man—no matter what Jonas said of him—was a threat to me. I felt suddenly as if I might faint. My head felt clammy, and the heat closed in around me. The stench of Con Trouseman's unwashed body rose in my nostrils and brought bile to my throat.

"Get out of here, and don't you come back, not ever!" The words were broken, but I managed to say them.

"You heard her, now get!" He let me go and I fell. I saw Trouseman running for the gate and Meg chasing after him, swinging at his head with the broom. He leapt the fence and dove for his horse.

"I've not finished with ya, Miss-high-and-uppity. Ya can't turn up yer nose at me fer no good reason. I'm the one to take the starch and vinegar outta ya, you'll see."

He jerked the horse about and rode off.

97

* * * * *

Alex wasn't up to walking that evening, so I went alone. If I'd been thinking straight, I would have realized it wasn't a wise thing to do, but my mood was dark and I longed to talk to someone, but there was no one. Alex was exhausted after working too long in the heat to clear the chimney. Clarey had had a bad day, and Charity and Jonas had only just returned from their two-day absence.

It was still hot—dark and yet uncomfortable. Not even night had brought relief. Of course, Alex would merely chuckle at my complaints and spin his stories about the way that life in such a place brought out the best in people. "When the way is too easy, most let up and get slothful. That can't happen here. There's no letting up or a man loses everything."

Alex was usually helpful to talk to. Unlike everyone else here, he didn't dismiss Grandmother Rachael's part in my life, but simply encouraged me to see her role in perspective. "We go about gleaning what we can from one another, but it's a mistake to emulate everything in one person."

Part of me had always known that Grandmother had been a bit of a snob, cutting people out of our circle simply because of their earning ability. It hadn't been right to do that. My weeks here had shown me how it felt to be cut out because of something you couldn't help. It wasn't fair, and it hurt.

Mel wasn't kind, and neither were Jonas or Charity and many of the ladies at church. The only reason I could find for it was that I'd had rich parents. Reverse snobbery—but either way, it was wrong. I could see that I must try to be more friendly and perhaps folks would forget about Papa's money and come to know me and like me as Alex did.

Lost in thought, I didn't hear the figure approaching, and when he spoke I cried out in alarm.

"It's only me, sweetie." My heart accelerated in fright, and I strained to see how far I'd come. Why couldn't this man just leave me alone? "I called at the inn just now, and that old Reiley gal said you liked walking this direction."

"I . . . I was just about to turn back."

"You should. You've come a far piece." But Trouseman's large frame blocked my retreat. "So you do this every night, do ya? You oughta let me walk with ya."

"That's kind of you, Mr. Trouseman." I thought it best not to anger him as I'd done earlier. "But Mr. Wubbleton accompanies me usually."

"Old Wubbles? That's no different than bein' on yer own. What you need is a real man—not the sissy spit-and-polish men you're used ta. Come on, I'll show ya a little grove what's right for cuddlin' and lookin' at the moon."

"It's been a long day, and as I said I was just turning back. Perhaps you'll walk with me?" I tried to sidestep past him.

A heavy arm came around my shoulders. "You'd like to git rid'a me, wouldn't ya?"

I knew it would enrage him to move away, but I couldn't help it. Contact with the man sent cold chills through me, and I jerked away from him.

He cursed, whirling me back around. "Ya won't go to the dance, and now ya won't even walk with me. Think yer too good fer me, dontcha?"

"Mr. Trouseman—Con, I'm simply worn out. I need to get back."

"An excuse, that's all it is. You won't give me a chance, but this time, you've got no choice!" His mouth was all at once covering mine—that leering mouth with its bad teeth and whiskey smell. I fought him. It couldn't be happening. My arms were pinned, but a flying foot caught his shin, and with a grunt he bent. I yanked away and started running.

"What's going on?" A male voice called from the darkness. "Who's there?" a woman cried out.

I stopped, whirling at the sound, only to collide into my pursuer's chest. His hand came down viselike on my wrist. "You jest keep quiet." His whisper was lethal. "It's me, Parry. How are you and the missus?"

My eyes focused on the shadows of a house. I made out two people on the porch—a man and his wife?

"Trouseman? You're not making deliveries this late?"

99

"Nah, walking with my girl's all. Havin' a little tiff."

"Help me, please," I got out before his fingers sent a shock of pain along my hand.

"You just shush, I told ya."

"Wait up, the lady's upset." The man left the porch and moved toward us. "How're you, miss?"

With the man just feet away, Con lessened his hold on me, and the blood shot back into my hand. "Mr. Perry, is it?"

"The name's Parry James, miss."

"Mr. James, would you mind walking me back to Clara's guesthouse? I don't care for Mr. Trouseman's company."

"No need to say that, Delores sweetie," Trouseman half-laughed. "I'll take you home."

There was a moment of stillness while the married man swallowed uncomfortably. He was smaller than Con. "She asked, so I suppose I'd better see to it, Con. Edna, I'll be right back."

"Nah, I said I'll see to it. You go on back to the missus. You know how it goes with women, Parry."

"Yeah, but . . ." he drawled uncertainly. "She seems upset and—"

I didn't wait around to see who won. I started back on my own, running like I'd never run before. I slipped once on the grassy bank of the canal, and my shoes, skirts, and knees were drenched with water. But I was up and running again, and as far as I could tell, no one was coming after me. When I stumbled up the front steps of the inn and burst into the door, Lyddie Reiley shrieked from the upstairs bannister.

"Goodness, child, what's happened to you? You're soaked." She bolted down the stairs.

I swallowed back tears. "Sister Reiley, I'd appreciate it if in the future you didn't tell unsavory men—"

She shrieked again. "I didn't think. He said you were expecting him, and I didn't think! Look what he's done to your pretty sleeve."

Her more sensible sister, Esther, had joined her now, and the two stood inspecting my dress. When I tried to pass, Esther reached out a hand. "You'd better tell Jonas. He'll see to it that awful man doesn't bother you again."

"Why the commotion?" It was Jonas, and suddenly both women were talking at once. "Wait, Delores!" But I charged upward, remembering his earlier refusal to help me against Con. I had no need of Jonas Luker's help—not now—not ever!

Minutes later he was outside my door. "Lady, open up. I want a word with you."

"In the morning. I'm tired, Mr. Luker."

His fist pounded on the door, and I thought it might splinter. "Lori, I can always get the pass key and let myself in."

"For once, Mr. Luker, would you heed my wishes? I don't want to talk to anyone." He growled something I couldn't understand, then after a moment I heard his footsteps retreating. He didn't come back.

I bathed my face and arms in the basin and inspected the damage to the dress. It was ripped beyond repair. If I had to, I'd take to using the gun Papa had sent with me. Nobody else was going to hurt me again.

Before going to sleep I wrote a letter to Mary Simms who had been our nurse and governess. She wasn't exactly a friend to me, but I had to tell somebody how awful it was here. Breaking my resolve for the first time, I wrote how unhappy I'd been. An hour later, I climbed into bed and blew out the lamp.

ELEVEN

Charity was especially kind to me the next day. She wore a softer expression, and when she saw me hovering at the door to her office, she actually blushed and smiled. "Oh, hi, cousin. It's a lovely day, isn't it?"

"Yes, Charity, it is. I'm sorry to bother you, but—"

"No bother. Is there some trouble in the kitchen?"

"Meg's a little late coming in. I know you don't like me doing the cooking, but I'd better get started or—"

"Oh, by all means go ahead. I'm sure by now you'll be much better at it." She smiled again and turned back to her desk, giving me the go-ahead to cook as casually as that.

By the time Meg had arrived I was finished, and though the food was noticeably not up to her standard, it was by no means inedible. The hashbrowns were too dark, the ham a little tough, but the eggs were light and fluffy and only a smidgeon oversalted. I braced myself for the barrage of complaints, but no one—not even Jonas—said a word. It was a quiet breakfast with everyone full of smiles and politeness. What conversation there was concerned the dance that evening.

As the day progressed, my spirits picked up some. The sky was overcast and cooler than it had been in days, and a blustery wind kept the flies away. Meg and I sailed through our morning work, and by ten-thirty I was free to comb Clarey's hair.

"I wonder what Dr. Hal would say if I were to turn up at that dance tonight?" Clarey mused.

"First he'd claim all your dances, and then he'd scold you good. There's not a patient in the area that gets more of his attention!"

A smile flicked over her mouth, and her color heightened. "He does take to me some. I think it's the way you've been doing my hair. I look younger, don't you think?"

"Clarey, you're pure Ashley—gorgeous through and through!"

"And so are you, my dear. What are you wearing tonight? I haven't heard you mention a word about it."

I knew she was shifting the subject away from Dr. Hallum. He was deeply attracted to Clarey, and despite her casual way of speaking about it, I knew she felt something for him too.

"I'm not going, Clarey. There, that does it!" I'd just secured the last of the pins at Clarey's crown.

"Not going? Why not?"

"Clarey, don't start. I'm not in the least bothered by staying at home."

"But why? It's a perfect chance to have some fun."

"I haven't an escort. I know I don't really need one, but I don't know people here, and I'm not about to wander in alone and be forced to suffer through the awkwardness I would surely feel."

"Delores, you could go over with Charity. She won't be tied up with the program all night, and you've met friends at church, haven't you? And there's Debra and Melissa—"

"Yes, I'm sure they'd do their best for me." I didn't add that it was the women my age, single and married, who were decidedly cool to me. Debra had suggested that this was my own fault, that my reserve put everyone off. Even so, I wasn't about to shed *all* my poise just to have a few faceless females befriend me. "Clarey, you're a dear to care, but I prefer to stay at home—really I do!"

"Compared to your life in Ashley, it hasn't been anything but a nightmare for you here—and it's my fault."

I scooped up the combs, brushes, and pins scattered over her coverlet and dropped them back into their velvet box. "Papa sent me down here to learn to work. He's determined this will not be easy for me. He hopes I shall suffer. And since it's his opinion that governs my return home, we should both be grateful I've been forced to 'slave.'"

I wrinkled my nose at Clarey's distress. "I'm getting better at it—slaving, I mean. Already today I'm done until lunchtime. And lunch will be easy today—just cold cuts, and the guests can help themselves. Then Meg says I'm free until three or four. That doesn't sound so awful, does it? So stop worrying about me!"

I blew Clarey a kiss, pulled a face until she smiled back at me, and moved out onto the porch. I sat in the chair swing and looked out over the white railing to the green picket fence and the neatly divided yards and houses of Clarey's neighbors. Why it was necessary for them to live in such an unbending climate escaped me, but they were to be admired for it. Alex was right to say I wouldn't forget the smell and feel of this place. It had a certain, inexplicable calm that was unlike the feel of any place I'd been before.

I caught the gleam of something on the front gate. It was the sweets box I'd given to Aldan, and it was sitting in the full sunshine, the lid on tight. I thought of the creature languishing inside and pushed to my feet. I didn't like to see the children gathering insects, frogs, and lizards only to imprison them to die. I picked up the container, holding the lid down tight to ensure that the frog or whatever was inside didn't leap into my face, and as I did so there was a faint scuffling inside.

"Aldan? Mara?" They were pulling weeds in the garden with Alex, and happy to see them working for a change, I called out a "never mind, kids" and decided just to find a cooler spot for the box.

I put it down on a crate against the side of the house, but the lid had lifted on one corner of the box. Again there was the rustling. Hammering on it to reset the corner, I upset the box completely. A huge blur of dark brown flew through the air and disappeared from sight. I jumped back, shuddering, and looked hard at the grass at my feet. It wasn't there. Whatever it had been was large enough to see easily, so I bent and brushed through my skirts to be certain it wasn't lurking in the folds of cloth. My flesh crawled in anticipation of finding the creature, but it was gone. I straightened and hurried back toward the front of the inn, but stopped with a jerk when I felt an unaccustomed weight tugging below my shoulder. The monstrous spider was clinging corsagelike to my blouse just below my chin. I screamed and tried shaking my arm and shoulder to rid myself of it, but it had no effect. I couldn't get the thing off without touching it, and I couldn't bear to do that. I cried for the kids, for Alex, wheeling my head away from the horrid thing. Its clawlike legs clung tenaciously to the thin fabric of my blouse. "Please," I sobbed, but the spider began crawling upwards, its warm weight touching my face. My knees buckled, and the world began to tumble . . .

"Delores, dear, are you all right?" Alex knelt above me, his face knit with worry.

I lifted my head out of his lap and tried to sit up. "Has it gone?"

"What, my dear?" He looked about in bewilderment.

"Aldan's horrid spider," I cried. But it was no longer on my blouse.

"My spider!" Aldan hollered. "What did you do with it?"

In a sudden commotion, Jonas, the Reiley sisters, and Meg all came striding toward us. Aldan hadn't stopped wailing. "I've never had a tarantula before, and she let it go!"

"What's happened *now?*" Jonas looked down at me.

"Fainted—went dead out," Alex explained.

"I didn't actually faint."

"She nearly fainted yesterday—" Meg put in.

"That was the heat, and you had a bad spell, too, Meg Gibbons."

"Was it that Trouseman man again?" Lyddie cried out.

"No, no. It was nothing." I tried to wave them all away. Why did everyone have to make such a fuss?

Aldan shoved his way to my side. "Lori, where's my spider?"

"A spider? All this over a silly spider?" Jonas groaned with contempt. "If you react like this to a spider, how can I be sure last night wasn't an overreaction, too?"

"I did *not* overreact last night. And any woman would be scared of a huge thing like that. It was right here—right on my shoulder—"

"There it is!" Mara shrieked, pointing to the thing lumbering up the side of the house.

Meg and the two sisters "oooohed" simultaneously and backed away.

"You see? It's not just a spider—it's monstrous!"

"It's a tarantula, all right." Jonas's tone had altered, and I could see he was impressed by the baseball size of the thing. "You may have been bitten, but they're not much more poisonous than, say, a hornet. So how did it get on your shoulder?"

"It's a long story."

"With you, I'd say it usually is." He gave way and laughed outright, and the others seemed to find it equally amusing. Each of them moved away—even Alex's eyes crinkled with suppressed laughter.

The children scooped the spider back into the box and danced toward us to show Jonas the hairy creature up close. My legs felt rubbery, and I wanted to lie down and pull myself together in the privacy of my room. I felt betrayed—not one of my friends had taken my fright with the least degree of seriousness. Tarantulas were terrifying creatures—hideous to look at. I'd never seen one before, and to have one confront me an inch from my face had been pure terror.

"Lori, Lori." Aldan raced up the stone walk after me with the box in his hand.

"Keep it away, Aldan." I ran up on the porch.

"It won't hurt you, see?" He pulled off the top of the box and shoved it toward me again. "They're soft to touch. Feel it."

"Don't!" I screamed, my control snapping. "Please, don't!" I burst into tears and, scrambling for the screen door, ran for safety inside.

"Aldan, stop it." Jonas's voice carried as I flew up the stairs. "You could see she was scared to death."

"You thought it was funny, too, Uncle Jonas," Mara accused.

"Yeah, you laughed first," Aldan shot back at him.

I shut my door on the voices and sank gratefully onto my bed.

* * * * *

"What happened?" Clarey asked minutes later when I took the back staircase down to her room. My upstairs room was hot in spite of the cooler day, and I wanted to get away from the inn.

"Please don't make me go over it again, Clarey. It wasn't anything, really."

"But you seem so upset."

"I guess I am. I'd like to borrow the buggy for a while and drive down to the river. May I?"

"If Jonas doesn't mind—"

"Cousin Clarey, must everything I do be censored by that man? If you don't want me taking the buggy, just say so, but don't always tell me to go to Jonas!"

"I didn't mean you couldn't borrow it. It's just that Jonas looks after things and you'll need help hitching up the horse—"

"Alex can help me, or I'll do it myself. I'm not a child."

"Go ahead, dear. But be careful—there's quicksand in places."

* * * * *

I stayed too long at the bank of the Virgin, staring at the brown water sloshing along the muddy banks. It was too much like home—the breeze, the sweet air, the wild grass and cool trees. But the sun finally reminded me of the lateness of the hour. It was five at least—and Meg was doing the supper alone.

I felt guilty and hurried back to the inn, but by the time I had unhitched and watered the horse, even the walk-in guests were leaving. That meant supper was over. Charity would be furious. But it wasn't Charity who met me at the back door.

"Where have you been?" Jonas glowered at me through the screen.

"For a ride." I pushed at the door, but he didn't budge from my path.

"I'd like to talk to you, Lady. We'll go around to the arbor."

"I really haven't time. Meg had to do supper alone, and it's only fair that I at least clean up."

"Trudy's helping, but don't worry. I won't keep you long." There seemed no escaping it, so I went along. No matter what I did, in this man's eyes it was wrong.

We sat on the worn bench, a little apart. "First I'd like to know why you didn't tell somebody where you were going. We've been worried. Do you think it's kind to up and leave without a word—or wise, for that matter?" He seemed to be making a special effort to be civil, but there was enough bite in his words to make me flinch.

"I told Clarey I was going to the river. I told her when I asked permission to take the buggy."

"You may have thought you did, but—"

"I know I told her. She said to be careful and that there was quicksand in places."

"Then why didn't she tell me? She only said you'd come in quite upset and had asked for the buggy."

"I don't care whether you believe me or not, Mr. Luker. Your opinion is not important."

To my surprise he nodded in agreement. "I think you've said that before."

"I'm not interested in this discussion." I stood. "Meg is waiting for me, and I'm sure Trudy wants to go to the dance."

His hand slipped around my wrist. "Stay put a minute. I haven't finished."

"Well, I *have.*"

"Sit down, Lori!"

Unthinkingly I obeyed. He took a deep breath as if to prepare for more unpleasantness and plowed on. "We haven't been getting along too well, you and I, and it's got to stop. This is a guesthouse, and we can't have family tensions disturbing the others."

"I agree."

"Good. We won't have any more trouble—not if we both try a little harder. I want you to know Parry James was here—and Edna too. I was wrong about Con, and I want to apologize to you about that. He won't set foot here again. I'll see to it personally. I hope he didn't hurt you last night."

"As you can see, I'm fine." I wished I could warm up to his apology, but for some reason I felt stiffer than ever with this man.

"He's given you a bad bruise above your elbow. It shows through your sleeve."

He still held my wrist with one hand, and one finger of the other traced over last night's injury. "I bruise easily. Now if you'll excuse me—"

"Dang it all, hold on. I'm trying to call a truce here. I've been wrong, and I want you to know things will be different now."

"Thank you." I would have gone, but Jonas still held my hand. He knew I was just waiting for the chance to bolt.

"Lori, look—as it turns out, I'm not going to be taking Melissa to the dance, and since Con's sure to be there, well, I think it would be best if I did take you after all."

"No, thanks! I'm not interested in the dance, and I most

certainly do not want to go with you. Now if you'll excuse me?" I pulled my hand free, and I neither stopped when he called my name, nor looked back.

* * * * *

The hustle and bustle of getting the children to bed and everyone off to the party had subsided, and the inn seemed empty now. I went out to sit on the porch to watch the fancily dressed couples on their way to the dance, their faces alight. Clarey had tried once again to induce me to go. "It isn't true, Delores Lyn, that you're not going because you don't have a date. You're feeling shut out, aren't you? I suppose my Charity isn't the only girl here who resents you. Am I right? Aunt Rachael would be furious—if she taught you anything, it was to keep your courage, to *refuse* to be intimidated. You should be going off in all your finery and show them all how a true Ashley behaves."

Perhaps I was conceding defeat by hiding here. I was passing up a grand chance to make some headway socially, but I couldn't go alone and take another snub. I just couldn't.

The door creaked, and I looked up to see Alex coming outside. "So here you are, watching the parade go by like Cinderella. I bet you'd like to go to this wingding, even if it has to be on the arm of an old man."

"Alex," I laughed up at him. "I'd much rather go with *you* instead!"

"Spoken like the grand lady you are, my dear. I take that as an acceptance?" And when I nodded happily, he continued, "Then I suggest we both make haste. I shall meet you back here in, say, thirty minutes?"

110   Thirty minutes—it was hardly enough time to do more than bathe. My hair had just been washed the day before, so I brushed it loosely about my shoulders and swept it back at the sides with pearl combs and left it at that.

I selected the frilly lavender gown Debra had given me, blackened my lashes, and dabbed color on my lips and cheeks. I was fifteen minutes late to meet Alex, but he didn't seem to mind.

"Ah, enchantress!" he exclaimed, straightening in his stiff-collared shirt. "I shall feel years younger just having you on my arm!"

Charity had taken the buggy, so we made do with the supply wagon. Alex let the horse plod along in a lazy gait, and we talked and laughed and sang our way to the hall. The night was full of magic and sweetness. This was a turning point in my life—I could feel it—a turn for the better.

TWELVE

The dance was well along when we arrived. Alex, charming and witty, more than made up for the cold stares thrown at me from a tight circle of girls who were clustered near the door.

"They're thinking it just isn't fair—" He gave me a bolstering smile. "And they're right. It isn't. Heaven has been very good to you—beauty, talent, brains. But then, they don't see the responsibility it carries nor understand that because of it you have to work all the harder."

We moved onto the dance floor in a waltz. "I don't quite know what you mean." I searched the dear, dim eyes. "Responsibility?"

"When we are given so much, we are also expected to give a great deal in return. It can be quite a burden for such little shoulders."

"Oh, Alex!" I wanted to kiss him. "You say the prettiest things. Why do you bother with teaching me, Alex? That is what you're doing."

"Why should anyone bother to polish a rare jewel?"

After three dances Alex announced that we'd have to find chairs. "I'm afraid the 'prince' is tired." His face was suffused with color, and he was breathing hard.

"Let's do sit and watch." I refused a rush of offers from

several males and sat back to watch the blur and whirl around us. But Alex was soon fidgety.

"You'd do me the greatest favor, my dear, if you'd go ahead and dance with one of these young bucks. Please! Go and have some fun and let this old man recuperate."

"But Alex, I'm fine. It's just as much fun watching, honestly."

"No, it's a waste of a beautiful girl, and it will take the pressure from me to see you up and dancing." He urged me upward as a young blond fellow approached. "Yes, yes, she'd love to dance."

I had no choice but to comply. I found the men charming and kind, and they hovered about as thick as the flies I'd shooed the day before. My unease with most of the women continued, though I talked with Debra and Mel, and now and then Charity. Most surprisingly, I found myself visiting with Melissa Stubbs. Considering my wicked maneuverings, she was quite kind, easy to talk to, quick to see humor, and really quite fun. Despite myself, I liked her. With all that wispy blonde hair, I'd judged her as empty-headed and fragile, but she was intelligent and strong in the gentlest of ways.

No wonder Jonas and Skeeter were so taken with her. I felt ashamed I'd interfered between Melissa and Jonas. It was obvious that Melissa loved him very much—it was in her eyes and voice whenever he was near. And poor Skeeter, seeing it too, was all the more anxious to assert his rights as Missy's escort.

Jonas hadn't asked me to dance once. But despite his physical aloofness, I noticed a difference in his attitude toward me. He no longer ignored me. While he hadn't made a move in my direction, I often found his eyes watching me over the heads of the crowd. My own gaze was drawn to his, and I unwittingly stared back. It made me uncomfortable to feel his gaze on me so often. After a time I tried pretending I didn't notice.

But *why* was he watching me? Perhaps he only wanted to

make me feel guilty for rebuffing him and then showing up with Alex. Well, he'd rebuffed me, and not at all kindly.

The dance went on and on. My nerves felt stretched to a fever pitch, and I was getting a headache. I felt those eyes on the back of my head. *Stop it, Jonas, stop it!* I whirled to confront him, but it was Con Trouseman standing behind me. I was startled. He'd been there all evening but hadn't uttered a word to me. He and his rowdy friends were on their best behavior. They'd donned their best clothes and manners, and though it was a facade assumed only for the festivities, they mingled easily with the Mormon community. Seeing me turn on him, Trouseman melted back into the crowd, and I was relieved that Con wasn't going to harass me as I'd half expected.

Late in the evening the music stopped to allow for Charity's floor show. Then Alex claimed another dance for himself, but he couldn't finish it. I was alarmed at his loss of strength. He was barely able to stand.

"I think we should go, Alex."

"Please, don't let me ruin your fun. Go on and dance." But I wasn't leaving him. I asked one fellow to fetch him a cup of punch, and another to open some windows. After a while he leaned over to pat my hand and smile, but I wasn't the least reassured. A chalky blueness persisted about his lips.

"I'm tired, too, Alex, and I want to go right now." I glanced at several of the men waiting to dance with me, hoping one would step forward and help me influence Alex to go, but they all just stood about with solicitous smiles.

"Alex, Brother Giles will help us out, won't you, Brother Giles?" But Alex wouldn't have it.

"Not yet, my dear."

"I think he ought to sit for just a few more minutes, and then I'll bring the wagon around. It's about time for me to leave too." It was Jonas. I felt his hand beneath my elbow. He leaned over to Alex. "Would you mind, Alex, if I took the lady away for a moment? She and I have something to do."

Alex whispered, "Go ahead. To tell you the truth, I would like a little privacy, and with all these fellows hanging about, that's been hard to come by."

"We'll be right back. Excuse us, gents." He ushered me through the several males Alex had complained about and onto the dance floor.

My relief at having someone take over the situation was such that it took several seconds for me to realize that Jonas was dancing with me. "Do you really want to dance with me?" I finally asked.

He cocked back his head and smiled at me. "Yes, I do. Now hush." He folded me into his arms, and we began to float about the hall. We danced two dances straight in almost utter silence, and they were thrilling! I did attempt to tell Jonas how much I liked his Melissa Stubbs, but again he shushed me, so I simply relaxed and enjoyed the hard arms that held me.

Less than thirty minutes later, we had Alex home. Jonas went in and helped him get undressed and settled for the night. After a quick visit with Clarey, I too went to my room and went to bed. It had been a long, exhausting day, and I had to be up early.

THIRTEEN

In years past my married sisters had made much ado about my deplorable lack of interest in children. They said I'd wind up another Effie Seach—an infamous woman who had little natural affection for her own babies. Her children, once born, had been handed over to her mother-in-law for rearing, and they were not allowed to stay any length of time in their own home until after their twelfth birthday. After that she seemed to assume a more normal role of motherhood.

But I hated it when Dorothy, Darla, or Denise made any comparison between me and Effie Seach. I knew myself, and if I had a problem, it was feeling too strongly about people, not feeling too little. I hadn't worried that I would ever be like Mrs. Seach.

Yet my engagement to Egan had changed all that. Despite really trying, I could not bring myself to feel close to his six children. They were good children, in need of a mother to love, but I was truly terrified I might end up as their mother. At such times my sisters' accusations came back to haunt me. Maybe I was another cold female like Effie after all.

Coming to St. George, though, had laid my Effie Seach ghost to rest once and for all. Though Mara and Aldan were wild, scarcely ever clean, seldom polite, and as quarrelsome as any brother and sister that ever lived, *I loved them*. I was surprised that I could be so concerned about two scrappy distant cousins, but I loved them with a love I hadn't known I possessed.

I found myself censorious of Charity because of her preoccupation with the inn and her problems with Randall. Her children were suffering. They needed a mother all the more because they were without a father. They each had problems that swamped them at times. Aldan was intensely shy, and Mara was much like me—she hung onto a show of bravado when she hurt the most. And she did it too well for a child. I began watching for it, hoping I could be close to her when she needed someone.

Then, quite by accident, I discovered something else about Mara. Charity, in her zeal for economizing, announced to the family that we must each have either butter or molasses on our bread but not both. I thought it a far-fetched measure, but I rarely ate bread, so it didn't much affect me. But the children were fond of hot, buttered bread dripping with molasses, so it was a difficult sacrifice for them.

After only a day of living under the new rule, Mara accepted her mother's decision without debate. At first I was proud of her maturity; then I discovered her tactic, which was an ingenious solution to her problem. Instead of setting her straight, I kept silent in admiration.

As soon as conversation at meals was well underway, Mara would butter her bread. Without biting into it, she would put it back on her plate, butter side down. After several moments, she'd take it up again, and as it appeared to have nothing on it, she'd reach for the molasses and spread it on thick. Flashing a cooperative smile, she'd eat her bread 117 in great content. Soon Aldan caught on, and he gave up his whining and fretting, giving the rest of us much-needed peace at the table. After a week or so, Charity realized the effort wasn't saving anything, and everyone drifted back to eating as he pleased.

The rule lagged, in part, because Charity's attention

was diverted by the presence of a new family at the inn. The Maun family, a bedraggled group—seven ungovernable children; a stern, unbending father; and a meek, bowing wife, arrived one Sunday evening looking for rooms. They came crashing through the door disrupting the music Esther and Lyddie Reiley were enjoying from the Edison in the parlor, and waking Alex (who'd been nodding in a chair) with a start.

As Jonas had gone off to work in Pine Valley for a few weeks, Charity consulted with me. "What do you think, cousin? Will they be as much trouble as they look?"

I hadn't known what to tell her. I knew we needed the money. Charity explained that we were nearly booked up, but that we had a tiny room upstairs. To her surprise, the father, Ian, said it would more than do, and all *nine* of them crowded into a space not much larger than my own cramped quarters.

Though not Church members, they were nevertheless very religious. At least that's what Ian Maun kept telling everyone, though his religion differed from ours as night did from day. He wore a perpetually mournful countenance and quoted odd pieces of scripture at every opportunity, and the passages he chose were not the ones I loved. To Ian Maun, everything was an "abomination" in the Lord's sight—including, and especially, joy. Clutching his worn leather Bible to him, he watched for every opportunity to teach and correct those around him—strangers, while, ironically, his own children were out of control most of the time. These he ignored or occasionally chastised inordinately. He wasn't a pleasant man, and I longed for him to move on as his wife kept saying they would do.

118   "We're just moving through," she'd timidly explain to no one in particular. "Just moving through . . ." And then once, as I helped bandage the knee of her youngest, she'd added, "Ian's looking for the right place to settle, but I don't reckon it'll be here. The place he wants is never where we are, but further along, a dot on a distant hill, a puff of smoke on the horizon . . ."

Though I did look forward to their departure, I couldn't help caring for Phoebe. She was a nice woman—at one time she had been pretty, and she was doing her best in a marriage that would have sent most into deep despair. Perhaps she was in despair, for while she was quick to smile with Meg and me, she never did in her husband's presence. She kept her head bowed, her eyes lowered. It was tragic to see.

One evening at the table, Alex had taken quite enough of doom and gloom, and he began to quote from the Bible loving passages that emphasized the spirit of the law over the letter, and Christ's new commandment to his disciples that they love one another. "Love and acceptance," Alex concluded gently, "is the foundation of all Christianity. Don't you agree?"

Ian Maun had drawn into tight-lipped silence, and had finally left the table altogether in hasty departure.

"The trouble is, my Ian loves a rule." Mrs. Maun murmured, without thinking, into the hush. "He loves a rule almost better than anything. I wonder what it would be like if he loved us half as much as his book there." And then, her mouth dropping with horror, she realized what she'd said. "Oh, my! You people must understand I love the Bible myself. I do! My father was a minister, and he taught me to be very fond of the scriptures. It's just that . . . I mean . . . I hope I didn't imply disrespect for the Lord's word or anything." Her explanation had been painful, for her small face became purplish and puckered, and as she hurried her children away from their half-eaten food and ducked up the stairs herself, I felt tears in my eyes for the life she had to lead.

Alex was right. I was blessed, and that night I spent a longer time than usual on my knees, thanking my Father in heaven for a gospel of love and for a prophet and Church leaders who emphasized the positive and joyful and counseled against fanaticism of any sort. And, too, I prayed for Phoebe Maun, a girl grown into a woman who couldn't at heart be much different than I.

119

Having a prophet of doom in the house casts a terribly long shadow, and the prevailing mood even in Clarey's rooms was one of soberness.

With Jonas still in Pine Valley, Charity's moods fluctuated with lightning speed—one moment she was serene and at peace with us all; the next she was snappish and tearful. I hadn't realized Jonas had lent such stability to the place. I missed him and watched for his return.

Jonas's absence, Charity's temper, and Ian Maun's ravings were not the only cause of my being blue. Papa hadn't written. In three long months my only news of him had been through Clarey and Debra, and it hurt.

He hadn't believed that my request for a loan against my inheritance was legitimate and wrote an angry letter to Clarey demanding to know if there even was such a person as Alexander Wubbleton and if he did indeed owe such a staggering amount to the inn. Clarey was swift to reply in my defense, but she also assured Papa that the inn could go along as it always had, without payment from Alex. What Clarey didn't seem to understand was that Alex couldn't. I despaired of ever getting the loan to him and allowing him to clear his debt as I'd dreamed of doing.

Aldan and Mara were also suffering from the depressed climate and even in a greater degree than we adults.

We were in our third week of Ian Maun's stay. I was working out back with Meg when I heard a loud scuffle going on. I moved to look into a far corner of the property. It was the Maun boys again! Already they had destroyed several new trees and torn down half of Alex's prized grape arbor. He had ordered them out of his garden in the most angry tones I'd ever heard the gentleman use. The next day they'd broken a leg off the outside table and had scattered soot and ashes through our neatly stacked supplies. While we were cleaning up that mess, one of the boarders discovered that the water collected in the barrels for bathing had been mysteriously drained. Besides all this, we had put up

120

with almost constant fighting, bickering, and boisterousness since the family's arrival. Seeing yet more trouble, I picked up Meg's broom and ran out to the scene.

I was horrified to see that the object of the tussle was a small decapitated doll. There wasn't much left of it, but still they fought, swearing, shoving, and pulling at the small arms and ripping the tiny eyelet dress. *Eyelet.* I searched about in the dust until I spied the china head. Mara's! It had been presented to her just weeks before by Clarey on the children's birthday. And even rough and tumble Mara had taken great pains with her new treasure. The doll had adorned her pink bed. It was her confidante, her playmate, her dearest possession, and now it was in ruins.

There was a sobbing under the boys' laughter, and I caught sight of Aldan watching, white-faced and tense, just feet away. Behind him was a movement in the dust. Ignoring the fight for a moment, I ran about to get a clearer view, and there, scuffed and dirty as her doll, was Mara, lying in a heap, her small shoulders rising and falling in silent distress, her tears puddling in the soil beneath her swollen cheeks.

"Stop it!" I screeched to the boys and began Meg-like to swing the broom at them. "Look what you've done! Shame on you. How dare you destroy another's property. How dare you!" The boys scattered and ran, and I cradled Mara in my arms. I didn't realize I was crying myself until Aldan asked if they'd hurt me, too.

"No, I'm all right, darling." I reached to hug him as well. He was trying to stifle a rising sense of shame that he'd stood by without so much as a mark on him and let them do this to his sister when on so many occasions I'd seen Mara fight tooth and nail for her brother. But then I supposed it came down to his shyness, and anyway, what could he have done? He had barely turned seven.

Still ignoring his sister, Aldan leaned to study my face as I dried my eyes, and my anger returned in a swift wave. "Aldan, why didn't you *do* something?" Maybe it wasn't my place to ask it, but I was shaken, and the words leapt from my mouth.

He looked to the ground. "There are so many of them, and they're bad. I . . . I guess I was . . ." he swallowed guiltily, "scared."

"I'm sure you were scared, darling, but you could have shouted or run for help. Meggie and I weren't far. Your sister needs you, Aldan. You're her brother—whether you are frightened or not, you should help her."

At that he began to sob, "I'm sorry, Mara. I'm sorry."

After a while we dried faces and blew noses, and I took them both to the outside kitchen and let them stir up cookies. I gave them the royal treatment the rest of the day, but there was no erasing the troubled looks on either face.

* * * * *

"When will Uncle Jonas come back?" Mara asked me for the tenth time one morning as Meg and I made lye soap in a big vat over an open fire.

"Never," Aldan muttered morosely. "He's gone away like Papa. He's dead."

"Of course Jonas isn't dead, and neither is your father. How can you talk like that?" I scolded, but then caught Meg's alarmed glance. I realized Charity must have told them Randall was dead! It was appalling, but it did account for the children's complete lack of curiosity on the subject. I bit my lip and tried to think what to say next.

"He is too dead, our daddy is." Mara kicked the dust hopelessly. "Mama says he's dead to us—and he is. He wouldn't just leave us and go off, would he? So what if Aldan is right? What if Jonas is dead and he never comes back to take care of things?"

"Sweetheart, he's in Pine Valley. He has other responsibilities—you know that."

"But he never stays this long—never!" She was suddenly close to tears.

"All right. Just to prove how sure I am that Jonas is fine

and only delayed with his business, I shall make a wager. Do you know what a wager is?"

Aldan was affronted. "Sure we do."

"Then I bet he will be back by Saturday—this Saturday. Cousin Clarey has had word from him, and I'm sure he won't stay longer than that. When do you think he will be back, Aldan?"

He shrugged. "Who knows? Maybe never."

"You don't believe that. You and Mara both pick a date, and we'll wait and see who's closest to being right. If I'm wrong, if he isn't back by nightfall Saturday, I shall make up an entire pan of nut cookies for you two to eat all by yourselves."

But neither child was impressed. "Nah—just cookies isn't enough."

"We have cookies all the time." Mara scratched her head. "If you lose, Lori, you have to do something we want. Doesn't she, Aldan?"

"Yes." He suddenly seemed to come alive. "We'll decide!"

Happy that my tactics were working, I went back with Meg while the two whispered together how I might pay off my wager.

"We've got it!" They jumped about with glee. "If Uncle Jonas isn't back Saturday, you've got to climb the biggest tree on the place—clean to the top!"

They waited with narrowed eyes for me to withdraw my bet. "Lori knows she's going to lose, so she won't do it."

"Of course I won't. I won't have to, because Jonas will be back as I've said."

"But if he's not—" Aldan growled.

"If he's not, I'll do it. I promise." The kids were delighted.

* * * * *

My wager caught up with me the following Tuesday. Jonas still had not returned. He'd been gone better than a month. Whatever his obligations to his brothers' cattle business, didn't he know everyone was concerned about his extended absence? The children were lost without him, and it was *his* fault I had to climb the infernal tree.

I'd begged for mercy, asking that I be allowed to climb one of the smaller trees in the orchard in the back of the inn—but Aldan would have none of it. He insisted on the corner mulberry that towered above the inn.

"Aldan, ladies of my great age do not do such outrageous things as climb a tree on the front lawn of a public inn."

"Hogwash," had been Aldan's response—a favorite term of Jonas's. "You're backing out like we knew you would."

"All right, all right. But you've got to find a way for me to keep my promise and not ruin my reputation. You and Mara watch for a time when the place is empty, and I'll get it over with *today*."

My main concern was Miles Lassiter. He'd returned in the night. I hadn't seen him at breakfast, but the Reiley sisters had been full of the news. What Mr. Lassiter did mattered to all and sundry! Just knowing the man was back on the premises added excitement to everything.

"Listen, you kids; once I'm up into the limbs, you've got to keep a sharp eye out and let me know if anyone, anyone at all, comes by. Promise?"

"We'll make Indian sounds—hoo hoo hoo." Mara cupped a hand over her mouth. "That will be the signal."

I'd been thinking more in terms of *someone's coming*, but if it helped to make it a game, then so be it. "And don't forget; you're not to say a word about this to *anyone*."

124 "Meggie already knows," Aldan put in.

"Yes, just so no one else does."

"And we've told Wubbles." Mara waited for my reaction.

"*Brother Wubbleton*, Mara," I corrected, "and you weren't supposed to tell anyone."

"He won't tell. He's promised, and if he does, he's vowed to tell them not to tell anyone either."

I looked from her to Aldan. "You don't know how relieved I am to hear it. Go on then, and check things out, will you?"

They ran off full of their plans, and after better than an hour hadn't returned. I was relieved they'd forgotten me and was enjoying lying in the grass in the bright morning air. I'd always been too concerned about my clothes to do anything like this before, but Mara and Aldan had changed all that. Now I romped and roughhoused, discovering a whole new world and loving it.

"Lori, Lori." They hadn't forgotten. I pulled myself up, brushed the grass from my hair and skirt, and walked to meet them. "Come fast, right now. It's the bestest time. Clarey's gone back in the house. She had two ladies with her on the porch, but they're gone." Each grabbed a hand to hurry me.

With the help of a crate, I was able to make the first branch.

"The first part is the worst," one of the children had chattered up at me, and I was happy to find it was true. The branches thereafter were closer together. I scrambled up easily, until well beneath the cover of the spreading leaves I could breathe out my relief. No one had seen. My heart slowed, and so did my feet and hands. I had time to think now. If I were quick, I could be to the top and down again in just a few minutes. My skirts snagged in the branches, and my soles slipped now and again, but I made good progress for a beginner. It was even kind of fun.

Occasionally I stopped to check the windows of the inn to be sure no one was peering out at me. Below, the children awaited my descent. 125

When the limbs began to thin, I called it good enough and started down again. Then suddenly Old Dog began barking up at me and scratching at the base of the tree. The children made no move to call him away, and I leaned out from a branch and tried to get their attention. All I could see was two little bodies rolling in the grass and writhing from laughter. I was about to hiss down a sobering warning when a female voice not familiar to me sung out from the gate, "Children, we're back. Help Clarey out here, will you?"

Then an onslaught of voices hit. "My, my, whatever is so funny?" "Let me carry that, Ethel." "Where, Sister Bergen? Out here on the grass?"

And then Meg was scolding the kids. "Mara, Aldan? Where are those chairs? Goodness, you've had all this time and you haven't even started. The Relief Society's here! And get that dog around back, quick!"

Out on the street was a clatter of hooves and buggy wheels. Women's laughter and friendly gossip drifted up to me. I was now high in the tree again, clinging to a flimsy cluster of branches that swayed with my galloping heart. *Those little brats had done this to me on purpose!* There had been talk of the ward sisters coming to pay Clarey a visit now that she was doing so well. They'd wanted to have a work meeting here on the lawn. Obviously, that was now commencing. Quilt frames were being arranged below, chairs hauled out. It would be hours before I could climb down. How could I stay here in this stupid tree that long? But there was no choice. I was trapped!

* * * * *

My back ached from sitting in such an awkward position, and despite my lightweight dress, the perspiration stood out on my face and neck. I was hot and miserable, and I longed for a drink of the red punch the sisters were sipping so leisurely below me. Some were gathering their things and talking about the next meeting, and I took some comfort from that. Others were moving into the cooler air of the shaded porch. How much longer must I wait?

I'd become so preoccupied with the women, I'd quite forgotten the threat of the windows. A sound behind me startled me, and I jerked around to see Miles Lassiter open-

126

ing the window and leaning toward me. It was too late to hide, but my reactions took over. I ducked to a lower limb, but it gave way with a crunching break. I was falling. In a blur I grabbed out at anything, leaves, branches, twigs, only to have them tear away and tumble with me.

I didn't hit the ground hard—perhaps the debris cushioned me. I knew immediately I wasn't hurt, only winded, and I lay supine with my eyes closed.

The reaction was one of hysteria. Chattering in high-pitched confusion, the women ran to inspect the damage, and speculation began about whether or not I'd fallen accidentally from the corner window or had jumped or been pushed. No one even suggested that I might have been in the tree, and when Mara tried to say so, she was hushed by a domineering female who said that she *personally* had been beneath the tree for three hours and hadn't seen me in all that time!

At last, because there was nothing else to do, I opened my eyes to see Clarey's own hovering just above me. "Oh, dearest, are you all right? What happened? Did Miles do this or did you fall from the veranda?

A woman with an ancient braided hairstyle clucked, "I never did like that Californian, and from the looks of it, he's made some improper advances to your dear little cousin."

I tried to sit up, but Clarey wouldn't let me.

"Look, she's badly injured." One of the sisters leaned to wag a finger in my face. "Her face is pale and wet. What are you going to do about it, Clarey? Throw the man out?"

"Stand aside, all of you, and let the girl breathe!" It was Miles, striding down from the porch.

Two women tried to bar his way, but he was through them and kneeling at my side before anything could be done to prevent it. "Is she all right, Clara? Miss Ashley—" His eyes were soft and dark, brown—no, charcoal, I thought as he studied me. "—are you injured?"

I shook my head, unable to think how to explain any of it.

"Are you sure? That was quite a fall."

"But it was my fault," I began confusedly, yet knowing I had to clear the man from the ugly suspicions being bandied about.

"No, no. It was entirely mine," Miles was quick to insist. "I shouldn't have let you lean so far out to see that silly nest. You might have been killed!"

"Nest?" I echoed. His eyes crinkled in response.

"Don't you remember? You asked to use my window as you couldn't see the baby birds from the veranda. I tried, believe me, but I couldn't grab you quickly enough. If you're hurt in any way, I'll never forgive myself." He looked truly stricken—except for those eyes.

It was the way out I needed. Miles Lassiter, bless him, was covering for me. I smiled my relief.

There was an answering smile on that beautifully etched face of his.

"I remember now, yes!" I pushed up on my elbows. "Oh! I wonder if I've hurt those little birds."

He shook his head, and a dark curl landed above one straight brow. "Now don't concern yourself with that. But you do look awfully shaken. I'll carry you into your room."

I wasn't sure we needed to go that far with it, but even with my protest, Miles swept me up into his arms. Clarey ran ahead, directing that Miles take me to Mara's room.

"It's much cooler down there, sir, and I'll be better able to look after her if she's close."

"But Clarey, I'm fine. Let me walk and I'll show you all."

"Not until Dr. Hallum has looked you over, you won't!"

"I think that's very wise." Miles winked at me and set me down, as if I were made of china, upon Mara's geranium-pink coverlet.

128   "But she wasn't looking at any old birds!" Mara groaned as if she'd been saying it all along and no one had listened.

"Shhh." Aldan yanked on her arm. "If we stay around here, Lori'll give us whatfor!"

"Did you two have something to do with this?" Clarey gave both children her sudden attention, but they bolted away.

"Something's not right here," she said, and went out into the hall calling after the children.

Miles, no longer suppressing his amusement, laughed heartily and then, leaning toward me, took my hand and, of all things, kissed it! "You know, Miss Ashley, you look like a duchess propped there against those pink pillows, and yet the only two times I've seen you, you were down on your knees cleaning my room and—today—outside my window scaling a tree! Incredible!"

* * * * *

After everyone had left, Clarey had a difficult time getting my shoe off. It seemed I *had* done myself an injury in the fall. My ankle was swollen and tinged with blue. Clarey sent Mara scurrying for the doctor.

As he poked and prodded the foot, I was dismayed to find it painful. I couldn't sustain my weight and asked how long it would take to heal so I could continue my duties in the kitchen.

"It depends entirely on the weather—entirely!" He grinned at our disbelief.

Clarey, impatient at Dr. Hallum's perpetual tendency to clown and flirt, shook a finger at him. "Hal, for once be serious. She's hurting."

"I'm telling you, doll. This all depends on the *weather*— on *whether* or not this young lady will do as she's told and stay off it. Not all my patients do as they're supposed to, especially those in this establishment."

"But we could wrap it, couldn't we? And then with some support I could walk—"

"There, you see!" The doctor threw up his hands in mock exasperation.

"Nonsense, Delores, you'll do as the doctor tells you. I've just been itching to get back into the kitchen. I can take over while you heal. Hal already said I can be up and about a bit, didn't you!"

"I was referring to light work, my dear Clarey, and you know it." The doctor scratched at his reddish beard, his

129

eyes twinkling with affection for my cousin. "When it comes to more than that, well, it all depends on the *climate!*"

Clarey raised her brows. "Oh, I suppose I can't *climb at all?*"

He laughed. "You're catching on, Clarey. No stairs. None! And keep the hours down, or I'll have you back in bed, and that, my Clarey, is no joke!"

* * * * *

"I beg your pardon, Miss Ashley." Miles Lassiter was standing in the doorway with several books under one arm. He gave me a warm smile and inclined his head so that the dignified gray at his temple gleamed in the light. "Clarey said I might stop in and chat with you."

"Of course, Mr. Lassiter. Please come in and feel free to call me Delores Lyn."

"I will, thank you, so long as you call me Miles. I understand you've turned your ankle and will be down for a few days. Perhaps you'd care to pass the time?" He gestured at his books.

"How kind. I'd love it. Please sit down, and let's see what you've got there. Poetry? How did you know I love poetry?"

He settled back into a chair, his eyes on my face. "Let's just say *I knew*, and I have a feeling, Delores Lyn, that I know a lot more than that about you. We have an affinity for one another, don't you think?"

"Affinity?" I knew precisely what he meant, but I was so embarrassed at his forwardness, and yet delighted, too, that I couldn't frame a reply.

"Yes, an affinity." I loved the meaningful glint in his eyes, the curve of his lips. "For instance, I'll bet money I can guess your favorite poet."

130

"All right, please try." I wasn't certain I had a favorite, but I was intrigued with the game, flattered that he'd care.

"It seems you'd be drawn to the romantic poets. You're a thinker, yes, but your emotions run high. Loveliness, esthetic beauty, true sentiment of the heart all mean a great deal to you. Am I right?"

I could only nod. What insight this man had—what sensitivity! And thus commenced a beautiful friendship. Miles spent the better part of two hours talking with me. We had great fun together, laughing and reciting favorite lines back and forth.

Because I'd missed my lunch, he had Meg fix us up some sandwiches, and we snacked together. Before leaving, he promised to come back to carry me to the dinner table. "You shouldn't have to stay here in this little room just because you can't walk. I'd be privileged to take you out to the dining room for meals or out on the porch to sit. Please feel free to call on me."

"Oh, I will, Miles! And thank you for the visit. Hasn't it been fun!"

"So fun we must do it again soon. I've a room full of books to discuss with you."

And then, glowing with the pleasure of knowing that this refined and educated man enjoyed my company, I thrilled as he kissed my hand once more in a grand gesture of continental courtesy. Not in all my travels had I encountered such a person. As far as I could tell he had the makings of an excellent catch, and wouldn't it be something to go home to Ashley on the arm of the urbane and wealthy Miles Lassiter? What a triumph! Wouldn't Papa be proud!

* * * * *

"So how did it happen?" I awoke to see a ragged Jonas Luker grimacing down at me. At least I thought it was Jonas. He was so unkempt and dirty, with several days' growth of beard, that with my sleep-fogged brain I wasn't positive right off. But it was him. His hair, soaked from the heat, had been flattened from the sweat band on his hat, but beneath its unruly darkness were those blue, blue eyes.

"When did you get back?"

"Clarey said you fell out of Lassiter's window and were knocked unconscious on the ground."

"Oh, I don't think I lost consciousness, Jonas. You know how these things mushroom." I ran a tidying hand through my tangled hair, aware that I'd been asleep and sure that I was a mess, but then Jonas hardly looked his best and wasn't at all concerned—worse, he smelled of horse and perspiration.

"The story's all over town. I thought I might find you here with a broken neck!"

Had he truly been concerned? "I'm fine, honestly. I just turned my ankle, that's all. I need only to rest it for a couple of days and everything will be back to normal."

"Good. You probably ought to stay right down here."

"Yes. Clarey's asked Mara to trade me rooms until Sunday. She's more than happy, and so am I. With all the windows it's cool and nice, and I love looking out at the trees."

"Yes," Jonas looked at the pink-trimmed room. "It suits you." He gave a little wave of his hand and began for the door. He was leaving. He'd been gone all this time; I was bursting with questions, but now that he was assured everything was fine, he would take no more time for talking.

"Jonas, there's something I want to tell you." He paused, his eyes lifting curiously.

"Oh?"

My mind was a sudden blank. Why couldn't he just stay a minute and talk to me as Miles had done? Why couldn't Jonas initiate some conversation? But he wouldn't, I knew. And anyway, it didn't matter. Miles Lassiter more than compensated, and my foot was hurting suddenly. I closed my eyes and tried to think. But I was finding that in Jonas Luker's presence clear thinking was an impossibility. "I guess I've forgotten."

He shrugged and went out, closing the door. *Ian Maun.* I could have told him about all that.

Just before dinner, Jonas was back. He looked his old self, clean shaven, all traces of black stubble gone. I was relieved to see the lean, hard lines of his nose and jaw again, and my pulse accelerated at his grin. I looked away, troubled at the pleasure of seeing him. It was Miles I was attracted to—Miles and his polished charm.

"Clarey asked me to carry you out to the table. She thought it might be more enjoyable for you to join the others. How about it?"

I put down the brush I'd been using and smoothed the cream linen dress Charity had just helped me put on. "You needn't bother with me, Jonas. Miles has already said he would carry me in."

"*Miles?* Miles Lassiter?" The easiness was gone from his manner, and he was plainly annoyed.

"He got back last night, I think. Anyway, he was by a little while ago for a visit and kindly offered to help me out. I accepted. Thank you, though."

He left the doorway, coming fully into the room, his chin jutting down at me. "Look, Lady, you tell Lassiter we don't need his help with family matters. I'm home now. If you need to be carried about, I'll do it!" And then, without waiting for an argument, Jonas picked me up. From the set of his mouth, I could see he wouldn't listen anyway.

FIFTEEN

No one was at the dinner table when Jonas carried me in. Mr. Maun was reading in the parlor, and he called out as we went by, "And he shall chastise workers of iniquity!"

Ignoring the odd remarks, Jonas set me down upon a chair, but Ian, his long coat flopping open, swooped into the dining room and repeated the phrase as if he were some vengeful minister.

"And he shall chastise workers of iniquity."

"I beg your pardon?" Jonas turned to confront the man without the slightest pause. "Are you addressing your words to anyone in particular, old man?"

Old man. Ian Maun came nowhere near being an old man. His attitude was archaic, true, but in actual years he couldn't be much older than forty. He was of average height and slight of build with a pale, sunless complexion and a long dour face. His brown frizzy hair sprung awry in the oddest places, and his closely spaced eyes were most often thin as slits, sitting beneath a heavy, scowling brow.

"I was talking to the girl there." He nodded at me, his strange eyes disappearing behind lashless, white lids. I felt a shiver jerk up my spine.

"We have no 'workers of iniquity' here, unless you're speaking of yourself. Why don't you just go back to your holy book there and mind your own business!" Jonas's low snarl made it a command.

"Are we not our brother's keeper?" Ian was slow to take offense. "This girl has been idling away her time the day long, playing about with children while others work, singing foolish songs, and, as I myself saw, climbing trees. It is a false story that she fell out of a window."

"Yes, I know." Jonas winked at me. The children had been quick to do their work. "But as it's her free day, she may do as she pleases!"

"None have the right to eat the bread of idleness, and the Lord's judgment upon her was swift and sure. She is injured, is she not?"

The family and other boarders were coming in now, moving around to find their places at the table unaware of the tense debate. Miles Lassiter had come in to sit at my left, accepting my whispered explanation with a shrug and a smile, and the Maun children and Phoebe were taking their places at the far end of the table.

"Tell me, sir," Jonas went on doggedly, "the two children she was playing with—did they look upset to you?"

Maun eyed Jonas silently, unsure of what was to come.

"Were they quarreling? Were they destroying property or in any way causing a disturbance to others?" At this point the diners quieted and began to listen with keen interest.

Ian slightly shook his head.

"And why was that, do you think? Maybe because they had some supervision? This lady was rendering a service— not only was she playing with the children, she was loving them, teaching them. Your own sons could stand some of the same. I'm not talking about your kind of harsh discipline, but loving attention, consistent training. Perhaps if your sons had more of that from their father, they wouldn't need to torment a little girl or destroy a carefully planted garden or chop up a table."

"Sir," Ian straightened, "that is not your concern, and I shall raise up my own as I see fit."

135

Jonas rubbed at his chin. "Yes, I'm sure you will, though it is a pity. But you will do it somewhere else. I suggest you try the Snow House. It has more facilities and can easier take care of a family of your size. Your good wife might be grateful for that consideration, sir, and so would we."

A charged silence filled the room, as if everyone held their breath in unison.

Finally, Mr. Maun spoke. "If we leave here, we shall leave the city."

"Fine, do it, but not before settling your bill."

Ian's face took on the first real color I'd seen in it. "I resent your implication. I'm a man of means, and I'm paid up."

"I'm glad to hear it. However, I'm speaking about the damages I've mentioned. I'll make up a list and settle with you in the morning. All right, Charity, Clarey." Jonas nodded at the two women waiting in the kitchen doorway. "I think it's time for the blessing. We're all starved."

* * * * *

My eyes opened to darkness, and I heard angry, arguing voices. As Mara's room was so near the entry, it was easy enough to understand what was going on, for the muffled shouts belonged to Jonas and Ian Maun. The man was skipping out. I hadn't considered he'd do such a thing—not with all his religious scruples, but it was happening, and Jonas wasn't about to put up with it.

I pushed out of bed and, forgetting my sore ankle, stood. With a gasp of remembrance I sank back on Mara's bed. If I were going to catch Phoebe, there was nothing to do but hop.

136   I pulled my flimsy dressing gown around my shoulders, took up the wrapped gift, and made for the door. The hall was dark, but a wall lamp had been lit where it opened into the wide entry. I hurried, clutching my gown about me and hanging onto the box at the same time, trying to use the wall for balance. My carefully written card slipped to the floor, and I had a time retrieving it. By the time I was at the front

door, it was over. Jonas stood on the porch, and in the shadows of the gloom Phoebe—head down and mumbling how sorry she was for the trouble—scuttled down the path after the rigid figure of Ian. Their wagon waited in the street. The silhouettes of the children could be seen bobbing about as they watched.

"Take care of yourself, Mrs. Maun." Jonas's voice carried through the night.

"Phoebe!" I cried through the screen. "Wait, please." At my voice she only hurried more.

"Please, Jonas, give this to her. Phoebe!"

"What is it?" He frowned at the package.

"They're going. Please, just hand it to Phoebe, Jonas!" I pushed open the door, shoving the box into his hands. "Tell her to please read the card."

Before I'd finished, Jonas had taken up the box and was running to the gate. The package was delivered just as the old wagon lurched away. Waving into the blackness, I cried, "Good-bye. Good luck!"

"What did you give her?" Jonas asked, coming back. His tone was dry, and I gathered he hadn't approved of my offering.

I answered defensively, "A dress of mine she liked— that green silk, the one I wore my first day here. She saw me pressing it once and admired it."

He moved up onto the porch, placing himself between me and the night. "I admired it too. So why did you do that? Ian won't appreciate it, and with all the dresses you own, why give one of your best?"

He was standing close now, and I reached back for the door. "To give something one doesn't want or no longer needs doesn't show sincere caring, Jonas Luker. I gave it to her *because* I loved it so much, and now Phoebe Maun will know that I love her."

I turned to hobble in, but before I was even aware of what he was doing, he'd caught me by the shoulders and was taking me into his arms.

"Jonas . . ." I whispered up at the dark face.

137

But he didn't hesitate. His arms tightened and, gathering me against him, he raised my chin and kissed me hard. Then, feeling my compliance, his lips softened as the kiss deepened between us. It was so unexpectedly wonderful, I felt a twinge of fear.

"Have you ever wanted to faint when a man kissed you?" Debra had asked me not very long ago, and though I had been kissed, I hadn't known what she was talking about. I did now, and I was scared. Jonas Luker wasn't the man for me. Papa would never approve. But just the same, my hands found their way about his neck until too soon, breathless, limp, and dazzled with an excitement I hadn't known existed, I found him scooping me up into his arms and delivering me to the door of Mara's room.

"Now go to sleep." He growled the order, his lips in my hair. But there was a flash of teeth as he set me down upon my feet. "And don't ever come out dressed like that again, little Lori, or there'll be the devil and Jonas Luker to pay!"

SIXTEEN

I couldn't believe it. Papa had sent the money I'd asked for—the full amount. I raced out into the yard to where Alex was weeding to tell him.

"Alex? Could you come over under the trees and have a word or two with me, please?"

He wiped at his brow and smiled. "I'm happy to stop, Miss Delores—happy for the excuse, and I'm hoping you've a mighty long speech to deliver. If not, embroider it some, would you?"

I laughed, my eyes on the dingy gray sky. "Look, it's overcast again! I wonder why it never rains. It blows and blusters about and the sky gets dark, but never once since I've been here have I seen it really rain down. Isn't it odd?"

"That's Dixie for you. Sometimes it seems there are no skies drier than these skies, and when finally they bless us with their moisture, it's a real occasion to give thanks. You'll see it come down, my dear, and I might tell you there is a stiff penalty for fussy females who complain about wet weather. So just remember that, lass. Now, what is it you have there?"

I'd forgotten to keep the envelope behind my back and so had to come right out with it.

"Alex dear, you've told me how you've tried for a loan

on your Idaho land. Well, something came through just now, and I'd be grateful if you'd consider it that loan you've been waiting for."

Alex opened the envelope with trembling hands. He stared at the amount for a moment and then lifted his pale old eyes to mine.

"But I can't take your money, girl. That would just be shifting my indebtedness from the inn to you."

"Alex," I began, looking for words that would not give offense. "This is my money, and it's only been sitting in a bank in Ogden. I'm making an investment the same way a bank does. When your land sells, I'll make a profit—the interest that will have accrued while you're using the money. Of course, it's up to you, but if you turn me down, I'll just go find someone else to loan it to."

His eyes reddened and I feared he would refuse me, but then he nodded. "I'm grateful. It was a fine, fine day when you first set foot here." He tried then to smile, but his lips began working so that he just leaned and kissed my cheek, and his brittle hand closed about my own.

* * * * *

It was a blustery day. The wind whipped about my skirts and pulled out my carefully wound hair until there was nothing to do but let it fly. We were in for a storm, I was almost sure, though I didn't say it aloud. Everytime I mentioned rain, somebody was sure to laugh.

I went into Zeke Hobbs Mercantile and hurried to make my selections. The windows of the store sighed and rattled, and the sky outside was growing lower and lower—an exciting, wonderful, menacing day!

140   After paying Zeke for my purchases—buttons and thread for Charity, ribbon for Mara, a stick of peppermint for Aldan, and the beautiful mirror I'd ordered for Clarey—I ventured back out into the wind.

There was grit in the air just as there'd been with the sandstorm, and I smiled, remembering Jonas Luker's whipping. It seemed long ago that I hadn't liked him—years and years ago. Everything had certainly changed for me. I'd never in my life felt such a bursting, uncontainable happiness. I loved everybody—everything. All the smallness in me had evaporated, and I felt grateful to the core that Papa had sent me here.

The smell of rain was in the air, and at the crescendo of thunder, I quickened my step, anxious to get back to the inn. The children would be wild with excitement, running about helping to close windows, and I wanted to be there—to experience this with them.

The sudden splat on my cheek was a surprise, nevertheless. There was another and another. Holding my package to me, I began to run as the sky opened and rain like I'd never seen before began to fall. Another shout of thunder rolled at me from the hills, and a jagged blaze of light terrified while it thrilled. "Gully washer." I'd heard the term from Jonas. I knew we were in for a real gully washer.

I ducked my head and ran, concentrating on keeping my skirts out of the mud and my parcel from falling to pieces. I nearly collided with a pair of boots coming out an adjoining door. I veered around the gentleman to move on.

"Whoa!" I was caught about the middle and hauled backward into the establishment. Looking up, I saw Jonas shaking his head. "Now who could this be?" He turned to the men sitting at desks and the several tellers behind their windows. We, obviously, were in the bank. Grinning, he shrugged and lifted a wet curl from my eyes. "Ah! It's Lady Lori out on a spree, buying pretties and sweets for me!"

Embarrassed at his loud teasing, I tried to shush him.

"It's quite all right, Lady. These people are your friends. They don't want you to wash away, and neither do I. You'll never guess why I'm here." He winked and took my parcel from me as I tried to straighten my soaked hair and dress. "I'm here to make a sizable deposit that came into the inn last evening. And I'll bet you don't know a thing about it."

I met his gaze unsmiling. It was nobody's business where Alex had got his money. "I don't know what you're talking about."

"Hmmm." He reached up and touched my wet head, tracing a rivulet of water down my cheek to my chin. "You're very convincing, honey, but it's no good. Alex got that money from you on the collateral of his Idaho land. He's already told me all about it."

"So?" I tried not to think about his finger lingering on my face and peered at the rain sheeting the windows, wishing the man grinning at us would just go back to his work.

"You've done a beautiful thing, Lori, but I hope you know that Alex's Idaho land was sold years ago for taxes. I've never told him about it because it helped him to think he still owned it. But the plain truth is, he'll never be able to pay you back."

Jonas could've told me it was raining outside for all I cared. "Then it will be a gift. Alex has given me so many."

Jonas grunted at my shoulder. "Your father won't find that a very practical way to do business."

I thought about that, wondering why I wasn't in the least alarmed, because it was perfectly true. Papa would be furious when he found out. I smiled and took Jonas's arm. "It's my money, and in any case, Mr. Luker, I'm not so worried about having Papa's approval as I once was."

He grinned and then almost as if he could read my mind leaned to whisper just before his warm lips met mine, "Good girl."

* * * * *

We took the long way home, laughing and tripping over puddles, stopping to shelter a moment beneath a tree or the awning of some business, and then plowing on again. Jonas and I weren't the only adults loving the deluge. Folks stood on porches, hollering through the misty racket and waving, laughing, slapping backs. Children, soaked to the skin, tumbled on lawns and chased about.

My shoes and Jonas's boots were soaked through, and our feet made funny squishy noises. As we came into the back door of the inn, I quickly inspected my purchases. The mirror was unhurt and so was Charity's thread, but Aldan's peppermint had run all over Mara's ribbon. Holding up the streaked blue satin and gooey candy, we laughed all the harder.

"Clarey?" Jonas sat down at the kitchen table to dry out in front of the stove, and we noticed for the first time the hush in the place. "Hey, Meg?"

"Where is everyone?" The inn was usually humming with activity, but not today. There didn't seem to be a soul around.

"Do you think, Lady," Jonas pumped his dark brows, "we've got the place alone?"

Unable to prevent it, I blushed. I felt like a schoolgirl, so pleased was I at Jonas's attention. Something was happening to me—no, to *us!* Surely he felt it too—it was there in his face, in his eyes when he looked at me.

Breathless, I went to Clarey's rooms and found her with her head down on her dressing-room table, her face streaked with tears.

"Clarey! What's wrong? What's happened?"

She jerked up, embarrassed at having been caught. "We've—we've had some rather disturbing news. Hal was here a bit ago. He was out to the Raines's place yesterday— that's Charity's in-laws."

"And?"

"Randall's been released. It's years early, but he paid back what he stole, and they've somehow let him out."

"I think that's commendable. It's good news, Clarey, surely you see that. Think what it will mean to the children. They think he's dead and—" But Clarey was shaking her head, and the tears were beginning again.

"Oh, Delores, if only you could understand this. You should have seen Charity. She went wild at the news. She's finally starting to cope on her own, and now she's got the whole miserable mess to face all over again. I don't know what we shall do."

Charity wasn't at home that evening, and neither were the children. Only seven of us sat around the table—Clarey, Jonas, Alex, Miles, the two Reiley sisters, and myself. The conversation was subdued, and as soon as the meal had been eaten, most drifted off to their separate rooms. Miles suggested that as soon as I was free I should meet him in the parlor for a look at Wordsworth, and Jonas followed me out into the kitchen and sat at the table there, talking to me as I worked. When I came to the pans, he sat me down and did them for me—every one.

The work was done and the skies had cleared some when two gentlemen in overcoats came to the door asking to see Charity. One, graying and balding, held his hat in his hands and stared at the door. The other—taller, leaner, younger, but with the same dignified look—met my gaze and with the merest smile introduced the one as his father, Chadwick Aldan Raines, and himself as Randall Raines. Charity's husband! The years had changed him (the swagger and arrogance I so remembered were gone), but he was still attractive.

"Would you kindly tell my wife I'm here to see her, please?" Coming from his lips the request seemed natural. He might have seen her only yesterday—not four years ago.

"I'm sorry, Mr. Raines, but Charity isn't at home this evening."

"Oh?" His head went back in speculation. He didn't believe me.

"Mr. Raines, it's true, honestly. She's been gone all afternoon and hasn't returned yet. Would you care to leave a message?"

"No, thanks." He turned to his father. "Pa, it was a wasted trip."

The older man asked, "Is Sister Casston about?"

"Yes." I was slow to answer, for Clarey was still very upset. I knew the last thing she'd want would be to talk to Randall. But feeling that the decision was hers, I offered them chairs in the parlor and went to find her.

"Randall's here with his father. Since Charity's not here, they've asked for you. Will you come?"

"Of course." She preceded me down the hall. A lamp was burning in the office, and I went in to put it out. As I did so, something in the straw basket on the floor caught my eye. Beneath the usual, crumpled papers was a neat packet of envelopes—a large stack, tied together with a pink ribbon. I pulled them out and set them on the desk top. The postal dates went back nearly four years. They were letters from Randall—written to Charity while he was in prison. Not one had been opened. Yet Charity had kept them. So why throw them all out now? It didn't make sense, but then maybe it did after all. *Charity was still in love with her husband.* Perhaps she didn't want to be, but she was, and his return had her scared enough that she was willing to deny her feelings by disposing of the letters. When the fears passed, she'd regret tossing them out. She'd want them back again, in time.

Feeling certain that this would be the case, I took them into Clarey's room and found a safe place for them on a high shelf.

After the Raines men had left, I begged Clarey to tell me where Charity was. She gave me a fleeting smile, and the weary look she'd worn when I'd first arrived was back in her large eyes. "Delores, my Charity is a mixed-up little girl right now. Dr. Hal took her and the children to Lorana Scribbs in Washington. Do you remember?"

"The woman who sewed up that lovely dress for the dance, yes."

"Lorana and Stephen are like family to us. Stephen was a best friend to Randall in the old days. Charity needs some time to adjust to this turn of events, and to find a way to tell the children about their father. Charity insists she won't see Randall, but given time she'll face up to it. She's got to." 145

* * * * *

Now that Alex's debt was cleared and he had some money to spare, his life took on new meaning. He seemed more energetic, was up earlier in the morning, and occasionally took me or Clarey for buggy rides with Old Dog chasing behind. He drove me out to Shinob Ki, the round, slant-topped mountain that the Indians considered sacred. We drove through the windy Washington fields and to the dam where the Virgin's waters were diverted into canals for irrigation. Alex told of the trials the early settlers had had trying to build the dam. The silt and quicksand in the river bed had refused to hold the hard-driven piles. The timbers had washed out again and again. "To build a dam on the Virgin," the settlers had claimed, "is like doing laundry. It's got to be done at least once a week."

One morning, hours before dawn, Alex took me out to Warner Valley, where I saw the beginning of the honeymoon trail. The soil was flame orange, garnished with profuse plants in riotous colors—turquoise blue sage, tall mesquite of the darkest green, pale green yucca, large clumps of yellow wildflowers—all backed by shockingly red hills. It was the end of August, the heat was engulfing, and yet I had come to love this place.

* * * * *

"Was that *you* singing in here?" Jonas poked his head halfway into the kitchen and craned his neck to see if anyone else was about.

"I didn't mean to disturb." Had my voice carried all the way to the parlor? A cattlemen's meeting was being conducted there.

"Disturb isn't what I'd call it. Go on, sing some more!"

146   I shook my head and avoided looking at him.

"Hey, I like it, really. Forget your work a minute, Lady, and sing for me."

The request seemed almost intimate, and though I'd sung for hundreds of people in the past, I couldn't imagine doing it for Jonas.

"You're not feeling shy, are you? The confident Lady Ashley, shy?"

"Oh, I'm not. I just don't want to sing, that's all." He'd fastened his hand on my wrist, and I glanced at it, then back into his shocking-blue eyes.

"I'll let you go when you start singing—not before."

"Jonas!" I laughed at his tactics. "You can't make me sing! I told you I won't do it!"

"We'll see about that. Come on!" He pulled me after him to the parlor while I protested all the way. I was wearing an apron, and my hair was a sight. But he ignored all my protests, saying I looked just fine to him and it was his opinion I should care about anyway, not that of a lot of strange men. Once inside the parlor, he announced he'd caught "the little songbird" but that she wouldn't sing. "Let's give her some encouragement, fellas; what do you say?"

At once I was surrounded, and it became apparent the only way I could escape was to go to the piano and sing. I was more comfortable in that gathering than I was alone with Jonas in the kitchen, so without too much coaxing, I went to the piano and sang a number I knew Papa liked. It was a rowdy sort of cowboy tune—the only one of its sort that I knew. I thought it would appeal to cattlemen, and it did. I got up to leave, but they insisted on another number, then another. It didn't seem to matter what I sang—even lullabies were heartily accepted.

Finally, I insisted on getting back to my work. As I made for the door, compliments rang out from all sides, but the best one came from Jonas himself. "Lady, you not only look like an angel, you sing like one, too."

"Thank you, Jonas." His arm slipped around me in a possessive way, and he grinned from me to his group.

"Isn't it a pity that she has to be so completely spoiled?" He groaned, mocking me. "What man can keep that up?"

I felt the smile flatten on my mouth and made a rapid departure for the kitchen. Charity was due any minute, and I still had all those towels to fold.

147

Behind me the door burst inward. "Hey, why'd you run out like that?" Jonas's drawl held a slight undertone of concern.

"I've got work to do." I grabbed the water bucket and ran outside. I'd never live my past down, never! Did I still behave like a brat without knowing it? It wasn't fair—I'd tried so hard. Jonas followed and took the bucket from me.

"Let me pump that water for you."

"Please, just go back to your meeting."

"It's breaking up anyway." He had the bucket filled quickly. "Come on, I'll carry it in."

"No, thanks. I might just stay out here for a few minutes."

"Hey, what's the matter? Are you crying?"

Why didn't he go? The mountains were blurring, and in a minute I'd end up disgracing myself—or giving him a piece of my mind. Neither would be any good.

"But I want to know what's upset you. You were great in there—they loved you. But you went running out as if someone slapped you."

"You really are a most thoughtless person, Jonas Luker. You really *don't* know what's wrong, do you? Just when everyone was being so nice, you had to ruin it. 'It's a pity she has to be so spoiled.'"

"Hey, I was referring to—"

"It doesn't matter. You threw cold water on me in front of them all, and then laughed at me. *Spoiled?* I work as hard as you do. How dare you throw up my past at me. Can't you see that my life has changed—that I've grown from what I was?"

He seemed stunned. "Lori, honey, I was only teasing you. And the guys knew it. Besides, aren't you being a little too sensitive? You know there's still a lot of the old pampered Delores inside."

"Would you stop it, Jonas?"

"Why should the truth—"

I grabbed the bucket from his hands, spilling most of it

in the process. "Here's a little cold water for you!" If the bucket had been fuller, I could have done more than douse the better part of his head and shirt. But then, afraid of what I'd done, I dropped the bucket at his feet and made a hasty retreat to the house.

* * * * *

Randall Raines came back every evening asking for Charity. After more than a week of being turned away, he became angry. "Miss Ashley, I know this isn't your problem, and you are doing just what Jonas and Clarey tell you to do, but I have a right to see my wife. In four years I haven't heard one word from her. You know where she is." His voice was low and controlled but carried a desperate note that tore at my heart. "Please, Miss, tell me where she's gone."

I nearly told him right then, but fear of Jonas's reaction stopped me. "Give me a moment, Brother Raines." I headed straight for the office. Jonas was there working. I explained my feelings in a jumble of words that brought him to his feet. "I'll handle it, Lori."

"But Jonas, we've got to tell him. This is all wrong."

I was near to tears, and seeing that, he growled, "Lady, don't think about it anymore. I know it's hard on you, but Charity needs this time. Just trust our judgment and stay away from Randall. He knows how to get 'round a woman—always has."

"But it isn't that way," I protested, hurt that he could think it was Randall's supposed charm that influenced me. But he was gone, and seconds later a thunder of voices and the crash of the screen door marked Randall's frustrated departure.

I tried to take Jonas's advice. I said a special prayer that the worry be taken from me, but felt no relief from it. Charity had been running from Randall for years. Clarey and Jonas had handled all encounters with the Raines family. True, Charity had been betrayed and hurt, but she was strong. She could have even me quaking with just a look. Had hiding out these four years made her happy? No, it had kept the hurt alive and raw. If only she could see that!

But Randall was proud too. He was contrite and aching to make amends, but another few days of this and irrevocable damage could be done. No man would humble himself forever. The schism in the Raines family might widen, never to be mended.

The next evening Randall didn't come to inquire after Charity, and I feared his attitude was hardening. The following evening was the same—no Randall.

"We've heard the last of him." Meg shook her head with conviction. "I can't believe he'd let them do this to him this long. How he must feel, standing there night after night, his hat in his hand—"

"Meg, where is the Raines place, do you know?"

She grinned, knowing what I was up to.

"Am I wrong, Meg? I've done so many dumb things—if this is another one, please tell me."

"I think you're right, Delores. This has gone on long enough. What are you all doing involved in it anyway? It's between a man and his wife. But my feelings don't hold much weight with Jonas. He'll be—"

"I know." I had to silence her right there, or I'd lose my courage. Jonas would be worse than furious. But if I thought about that too long, I'd back out.

I didn't even have to ride to the Raines's place. Meg had seen Randall riding by on horseback with David Holliver just moments before. "He's still there, I'll bet. David works at the bank, and word is that Randall might be going back to work there."

150   I went right then, and when it was done and Randall was on his way to Washington, I went to confess to Jonas, praying he'd understand and forgive me.

"You did what?" He charged out of his chair.

"I told Randall that Charity's at Lorana's in Washington."

He looked at me, his eyes blazing. He took several steps toward me. "What gave you, *of all people,* the right to do that?"

"I—I—" Finding words to defend myself was difficult, I was so stunned at the black hostility in his eyes. He looked ready to kill.

"But Jonas, Randall might have found out from anybody, and he had to be told. I thought it would be best. I—"

"You thought! *You thought!* Why don't you just do as you're told, Lady?" His lips curled in a sneer around what had become a fond nickname, but no fondness was evident in his voice. I felt as though my world were dropping away beneath me. "I hope you haven't ruined everything!"

"Don't you see, I only wanted to help Charity."

"Be still!" He wheeled back to the desk and began slamming drawers in a frantic search for something. "She hasn't been exactly kind to you, has she? And you're feline, too. Maybe it does make a lot of sense."

I felt as though he'd hit me full in the face. Vindictive, feline—he couldn't be more wrong. I hadn't done this to hurt Charity. I admit I'd done some catty things before— had even gotten deliberately lost once on a family picnic to repay my sister for a supposed humiliation. Perhaps Jonas was right. He seemed to see right through me—perhaps that awfulness was still inside me and I was unaware of it.

I went to the back door and watched Jonas as he rode out. Obviously, Randall Raines wasn't the only one going to Washington tonight.

"I gather he didn't take it too well," Meg said.

"No."

"He'll get over it—just give him a few years." She chuckled at her ill-timed joke, then patted my shoulder. "Sorry, Lori. I know how he can be. Jonas really ought to do something about that bad temper of his."

I waited up for Jonas's return. Sleep seemed impossible until I was sure things would be all right. But soon after two in the morning, I fell asleep.

151

SEVENTEEN

"I understand Tuesday is your day off," Miles Lassiter said as he came into the kitchen the next morning.

"Hi, Miles." I forced myself to be cheerful, knowing how men hated a woman to go grumbling about. "You're looking awfully good."

He gave me a wink, his handsome face lighting up with a disarming smile. "I'm glad you said that, Delores Lyn. So am I mistaken? Don't you have today to yourself? It is Tuesday."

"Oh, she's free to go." Meg banged a pot down onto the stove. "Trouble is, Mr. Lassiter, I can't *drive* her out. Maybe you can convince her to take her hard-earned day and do something *fun* with it. She could use some cheering up." A matchmaking glitter lit her eyes as she looked at the two of us.

Miles picked up Meg's blatant hinting with the air of one well accustomed to turning a situation to his own advantage. "Well, as it happens, I do have something *fun* in mind, and, Mrs. Gibbons, with your help, I'm sure I can persuade this lovely lady to join me. I must say she's always been able to come up with an excuse in the past."

The "something fun" Miles had in mind was an outing to Harrisburg. He had to deliver some papers there, and on the way we stopped at a wayside creek and, spreading a blanket beneath a stand of cottonwoods, had a picnic.

"Your Meg Gibbons is quite the cook." Miles helped himself to a second piece of apple pie.

"Yes, she is. She's trying to teach me how, but I think as far as good cooking goes, I'm a slow learner—maybe an impossible one."

"A woman who looks like you, Delores Lyn, doesn't need to know how to cook." It was a pretty compliment, but it hit me wrong.

"Of course I do. A woman who can't cook properly is like a man who can't provide for his family. It's a basic role for a female—an essential." I sat up and began repacking the picnic basket.

"I suppose you get all this old-fashioned philosophy from that church of yours." He said it off-handedly and I answered in the same way, but he stared intently at me.

"I guess I do, yes." I rewrapped my half-eaten sandwich with more care than was necessary. It was the ideal time to talk to him about the Church. Hadn't I been just dying to do some missionary work with him? The only possible objection Papa would have to Miles was that he was a non-member. He was intelligent and sensitive, without any encumbering worldly habits as far as I knew. Joining the Church should be natural for him.

"What's the matter, Lori?" He ran caressing fingers up my bare arm. It was the first intimate overture Miles had made, yet I found myself regretting it. Why? He was everything I wanted, wasn't he? I loved his looks and his manners. He was educated, articulate. We shared so many of the same interests. I had only to get him baptized, and the rest of my life would be smooth sailing. I could go on with all the former ease of my old life. I would have the luxury and peace of mind that only a man of position could give.

"You've got a little thundercloud hanging over you today, love. Something's upset you, and you must tell me about it so I can fix it for you."

153

It was dear of him to care, but I couldn't confide family matters to him. I sniffed back gathering tears and tried to smile. "It's just one of those days, Miles. I'm all right, really."

"No." His kind eyes studied me. "Someone's hurt you, and I insist you tell me about it. I can't help unless I know what's happened, can I?"

"It isn't what you think, Miles. *I've hurt someone else.* I thought I was helping them, but as it turns out it was a terrible mistake, and I'm afraid I won't be forgiven." At that I started to cry.

Miles gathered me in his arms and held me a long while, hugging my head against his solid shoulder. It was just a shame that I hadn't fallen in love with Miles Lassiter before getting so heart tangled with Jonas.

* * * * *

After my cry I felt better. I was able to forget my problems somewhat and enjoy the day with Miles. He knew the art of engaging conversation, and before I knew it, dusk was settling in and we were pulling up in front of the inn. It had been a beautiful ride, and full of gratitude for Miles's thoughtfulness, I happily thanked him as he lifted me down from the carriage.

"It was my pleasure." He did seem satisfied with our day. "And now, if I may see you inside?" He gave me his arm, and together we began up the path. I broke a step when I spied Jonas standing on the porch, arms folded, watching us. Mara and Aldan were playing on the side lawn, so Charity obviously was back. Dying to know how things had worked out, I lost track of what Miles had been saying.

154

"Will you?" His eyes met mine.

We were now within feet of Jonas, and embarrassed at not having heard the comment, I could only stammer about.

Helpfully he repeated himself. "I was saying, love, that

if you need another shoulder to cry on, remember that mine works just fine, will you?"

I laughed. "Yes, thank you, Miles. I hope I didn't spoil things for you. I loved meeting your friends in Harrisburg."

"And they loved you, so we'll go back again soon, won't we." Miles nodded at Jonas, and I smiled at him, but he averted his head as we passed.

Jonas was still angry, obviously. I had a pain in the area of my heart, but trying to seem happy, I laughed at something Miles was saying and went with him inside the inn.

Following dinner that night I went straight to Charity and apologized. "I'm sorry, Charity, for having done that. I . . . I meant to help, but Jonas was terribly angry. I won't forgive myself if I've made your life any harder than it already is.

"Won't you?" she laughed tonelessly, her eyes tragic. "Oh, Delores, you haven't hurt a thing! It was silly of me to run like that in the first place. I had to talk to the man sometime. Randall knows now how things stand, and he won't be back. It was all really very simple. So you see, I ought to thank you. Your interference forced me to tell the children. They know now they have a father. We'll get through this, *my* children and I. Don't worry."

But I was worried, and not just for Aldan and Mara. I was worried for their parents and didn't know how in the world to help them.

* * * * *

The following Sunday Miles shocked me by asking to attend church with me. In all our talks he had avoided the subject of religion, and whenever we hit upon something that was close to my heart like children, or temple marriage, or life hereafter, he had been rather cynical. I'd felt a rather gaping gulf of incompatibility between my dedication to the Church and his unbeliever status.

So it was with mixed enthusiasm and trepidation that I

155

went off to church with him Sunday. He rented a new buggy, and we rode together in that. It was stake conference, and of that I was glad, for conference generated a special spirit and would give Miles an opportunity to hear the best speakers.

Alex had cornered me shortly after breakfast Sunday. "Mr. Lassiter is a fine man, lass. But don't be too disappointed if he doesn't feel what you feel. Thinkers rely much on themselves, on their abilities to think and reason. And the gospel works in the heart and not just the head."

I had taken special pains with my appearance. I went through my trunks and found an ice-blue Swiss dress with a sophisticated hourglass cut and a tiny overskirt at the hips. A parasol and blue feathered hat completed the outfit. I wore my hair up in the curls that Grandmother had loved best. It was the former me again, an image much more suited to the dashing Miles Lassiter.

The tabernacle was impressive, as always, and the trees and lawns were elegantly cared for. I felt proud of the stately and sacred building. We took a seat in the side pews under the balcony. Open windows to our left kept us cool.

Miles seemed uninterested in the singing. Though I pointed out the words in the hymnal, he wouldn't join in, so I sang without him. He seemed unresponsive during the entire service. After the closing prayer, we walked out beneath the trees, and he suggested we walk for a while before going back to the inn.

"All right, Miles. Did you enjoy the meeting?"

"Blue is your color, Delores Lyn."

"But did you enjoy the meeting, Miles? The speakers were marvelous, weren't they?"

He took a long time to answer. "I was impressed," he said finally. "Quite impressed."

I'd been positive he'd been about to say something very different, and so felt quite relieved. But when I tried to discuss some of the talks we'd heard, Miles once again switched subjects. I let it drop. We'd made a first step. I shouldn't rush him.

EIGHTEEN

I lay listening to the rain hitting the roof just above my head, then falling in a noisy stream outside the blackness of my window to puddle on the ground below. Dawn seemed far away.

They did this to me, the nightmares, filled me with a nameless foreboding that couldn't be real. Everything was fine at home—fine here. I sat up and pushed out of the bed. It did no good trying to sleep; what I needed was a walk to dispel this gathering depression.

Dressed in a cape and boots and armed with a lantern so I could see my way through the gray drizzle, I let myself out the back and padded across the soggy grass to the gate.

Everything was in such a muddle. I couldn't seem to make up with Jonas, and I'd begun to believe that he *wanted* it this way. Maybe it had been wrong of me to help Randall, but even so, it didn't justify Jonas's overnight withdrawal from me. Jonas was now painfully polite, careful to say only the right thing, and he was as distant as the moon.

At the same time Miles Lassiter was drawing closer and closer, attending Sunday School and sacrament meetings with me each week. He had even mentioned his intention of joining the Church. In this, at least, I could find some satisfaction. It was my first missionary effort, and yet it was happening so easily. How rewarding it was to introduce someone to the blessings of the gospel, and if this came through for him, the man wouldn't have a flaw. Miles was never moody. He intuitively sensed what a woman found attractive in a man. He was bold and firm, and yet not overbearing; he was thoughtful, but never ingratiating or weak; and he had a knowledge of the world but was in no way coarse or low-minded. He was, as Meg had said, "quite dazzling!" And he was seriously courting me. I knew because he'd told me so.

"I hope you understand, Delores Lyn, that I've every intention of winning you." With all the little attentions a man can show a woman, he was expertly carrying out his campaign. It made little sense, but *I was frightened.* Contrary to Jonas's critical opinion of my upbringing, Miles found it above reproach. And what confused me all the more was that I knew Jonas had been right when he said that deep down a lot of the old Delores was left. I still yearned for the beautiful, finer side of life. Even after learning the merits of hard work and the virtues of thrift, I contrarily looked for an easier existence than either of my cousins knew here at the inn.

What was wrong with having money? It brought freedom, peace, security—and while I might no longer live and breathe for Papa's approval, still it meant *something.* I couldn't understand why the loss of Jonas's friendship had depressed me so. It had meant much—the teasing and light-hearted camaraderie had filled a void, but obviously it hadn't meant that much to Jonas. I had to pick up my chin and appreciate what I had.

Marriage to Miles would be a breeze. His age was of concern—he was much older than I, but he was young in attitude. He was a fascinating man and always would be. Only last night he had kissed me, and it had been wonderful. I wanted him to kiss me again, to ignite those feelings that were somehow missing. *Why didn't he grab me and kiss me with the ruthlessness I'd seen in Jonas's eyes?* But Miles was a gentleman and far removed from Jonas's rugged world.

Thoroughly soaked now, I shivered a little but kept on. I couldn't escape Charity's troubles, either.

Randall had given up on her, though not on the children. He called at the inn nearly daily, and despite Charity's attitude, Mara and Aldan waited and watched for his visits with enthusiasm.

I'd overheard a painful scene between Randall and Charity late one night. I was trapped in the bathroom as they fought it out in the kitchen. Charity had reiterated her stand, that she could never forgive her husband. He could try until doomsday, but it was hopeless. He had taken something beautiful and crushed it, had ruined all their lives, and she could never forget it or forgive him!

"You're misnamed, aren't you? I've said I'm sorry for four long years—how much longer must I say it? I've lived on my knees and followed the counsel of my bishop. I've asked forgiveness of you, my children, and the people of my ward. I've repaid what I took. I know I was wrong, but I've paid for my mistake and others are forgiving me. Mr. Carrington has offered me my old position at the bank. He trusts me, don't you see that? I want to pick up the pieces and make something decent of myself. Folks here believe in repentance and forgiveness—everyone except my own wife."

He had gone out, leaving Charity crying.

The rain let up some, and it was graying in the east. I had to get back.

* * * * *

"What's the matter with me?" Was Charity talking to *me*? It wasn't like her to, not when it didn't relate to the kitchen work, but as no one else was in the dim kitchen, I looked up in response. I'd just come from the bathroom and was drying my hair.

"I don't know what you mean, cousin."

"What's the matter with me, Delores? Jonas says I've changed, lost my perspective. He thinks I'm all wrong about Randall. But I feel like the sheriff just took him away yesterday. *It wasn't four years ago to me!* The *trial* and the *humiliation are still happening,* and my life's been ripped from under me. I can't forgive him for what he's done—I never shall. Is that so hard for everyone to understand?"

Tears were welling up in her eyes, and I put a hand on her shoulder. "Oh, Charity. I don't know enough about it to help you. I wish I were smarter."

"Why is it so easy for everyone else though?" She dropped into a chair and buried her head in her hands.

"I suppose, well, because they weren't married to him." After a moment I went back to my hair and, brushing out the tangles, moved to the stove to dry it out.

"Did you know, Delores, Jonas once loved me very much. He even asked me to marry him, but I was already in love with Randall. Randall was so flashy and confident, and Jonas had been my big brother all my life. I just hadn't felt about him in that way. But when Randall betrayed me, I looked at Jonas and felt like a fool. I could have had him, and it would have made all the difference. Jonas has been protective ever since, but now even he's on Randall's side. He wants me to go back—to forgive him. He said that Randall's got his head on straight now and that he likes him." She half-laughed. "Imagine that. At one time they were bitterest enemies."

"Charity, I've an idea that might help. Excuse me and I'll be right back."

She shrugged, unimpressed as I left the room, but when I returned with the packet of letters in my hand, I had her attention. Her expression hardened.

"Now don't get angry, Charity." I tried to reestablish what little rapport we'd shared. "You've asked me what is wrong. You say you feel as though it all happened yesterday, but why?"

"I suppose you're going to tell me?"

"Time has gone on, cousin, but you haven't kept up with it. You stopped your relationship with your husband when he was convicted. You haven't given yourself an op-portunity to work through it, and maybe if you read through these letters of Randall's you might find that your attitude could begin to change as his changed. It's worth a try, isn't it, Charity?"

She sat there, her mouth growing smaller as I spoke. And it was apparent that again I'd done the wrong thing. Fuming, she stood and moved toward me. "Where did you get those?"

I stuttered, "They . . . they were in your wastebasket, and I . . . Charity, I was sure you hadn't meant to destroy them."

"But I did. How dare you touch my personal letters!" She snatched them from my hand and threw them with a vengeance into the open grate of the stove. I grabbed them out, but the bottom envelope had caught fire on the corner, and I beat it out with my hands.

"Give them back." She reached again to take them.

I flung myself away. "Charity, these represent four years of a man's life."

"They're not your property!"

"All right, burn them—but not before you've at least read them. You owe that to Randall."

"I don't owe him a thing—*not a thing!*"

I made one last try. "Maybe not. But you do owe it to the children, and to yourself, Charity! It's really just fear, isn't it? You're scared stiff you might begin to understand, and *you don't want to. Why?* Does it give you a feeling of power to hold an ax over Randall's head like this?"

"Why you stupid, interfering—" She dove toward me.

The dining room door swung inward, and Jonas stood there, huffing for breath, his hair and clothing soaked through from the rain. I was grateful for the interruption. It would give Charity a minute to think. In this, at least, I *was* right.

"Good morning, Jonas." I smiled and stepped around my cousin, clutching the packet of letters in trembling

161

hands. The argument had left me shaken, and I failed to notice that Jonas hadn't returned my greeting. Neither did I notice how odd it was that he'd come through the front way when his boots were so dirty. But when I glanced at him again, I could see he was more than wet—he looked ill, pale about the lips, with a dull, glazed expression in his eyes.

Ignoring Charity, who was still glowering, her condemning eyes on the bundle I held, I asked Jonas if he were all right.

He half-turned from me, pushing a hand over his mouth and then up the side of his face to rub his eyes in a gesture of utter weariness.

"Jonas—"

"I've got something to tell you both. Maybe you should sit down."

"Oh, what is it now?" Charity asked with scathing impatience. "A complaint?"

"It's . . . it's Wubbles—Alex. Uh . . . he left early this morning—"

"To find my wandering cousin, yes, I already know." Charity thrust her chin at me, and the frown line between her eyes deepened. "He told me he'd seen 'Miss Delores,'" her emphasis was waspish, "going out in the rain in the night, and as she hadn't returned he was worried. Well, I've done that for years—gone walking at all hours, and Wubbles hasn't so much as inquired why. Our 'Miss Delores' here can certainly cast a spell, can't she!"

"Let me finish, Charity." Jonas cut her off gently. "I'm afraid that Alex has had a heart attack. Quinton Hobbs found him down by the temple—"

"Alex? No! Where is he?" I could see him, lying on the cold ground there in the rain, waiting for me to come. I started for the door, but Jonas caught me around the middle.

"Easy, honey, easy. He's dead, Lori. I've just seen him. I'm so sorry, but he's gone."

A horrible wail rose up inside me, and with it pain, soul-deep, unlike any I'd known. Not Alex—*not my Alex*. I fought Jonas, pleaded with him, but he wouldn't let me go. Didn't he know I had to run and find him—to see Alex's dear face and touch his hand once more? I had to talk to him, and thank him, and wish him farewell, and tell him to take care . . .

"I love you Alex, I've never told you, but I love you." It couldn't just be over. He was a part of me—my dearest friend, and I'd just found him. He wasn't dead. He could never, never be dead. No one—not Jonas—no one would be able to make me believe it.

"He was looking for you!" In a daze my mind was repeating the accusation, but it was Charity's mouth that moved. "He died looking for you, don't you see? It's your fault. He was too old and sick to go out in such a storm. It's your fault!"

And though Jonas turned on Charity, telling her for once not to be a shrew, I knew it was true—horribly true. Alex!

NINETEEN

"So are you coming with me in the morning?" I was on the upstairs veranda. The fields darkened in the haze of evening, and below in the shadows of the garden, I watched, half-wishing to see the small form of an elderly man shuffling toward the house.

"I beg your pardon?"

Jonas sat on the railing with his foot hitched up, his eyes on my profile. "This is a new haunt for you. You sit here every evening now."

I nodded, my gaze shifting to the red bluffs. "I like to say goodnight to the hills. Alex did that, you know, and he said no matter where I went, I would remember the smell and feel of this place with the night coming down."

"Lori, you've got to stop mourning him, honey. He lived a good, long life. The only sad thing about his dying is that we here miss him. Alex has been alone for more than twenty years. You can bet *he* isn't downhearted. No, he's probably celebrating with Lillian in grand style!" He gave me a bolstering smile. "Lori?"

"I know, Jonas." And I did. My *mind* knew very well that Alex was happier where he was with his wife and daughter, free to move about without the confinement and pain his old body had put upon him, and yet my *heart* continued to miss him. I felt thrown back into all the grief of Grandmother's death. It had taken so much from me—death had—those who'd loved me best: my mother, my grandmother, and now Alex. Did one always just go on?

"Well then, are you coming to Pine Valley with me and the kids?" For more than a week since the funeral, he and Clarey—even Charity—had been working on me to go. "I've just got word back from Norene and Aaron, and they're looking forward to meeting you and having the children up there again. And you've got to know that Charity's counting on this time to be alone some with Randall without the kids underfoot."

That wasn't the real reason they were all so anxious to have me go. Even with the kids "underfoot," Charity had made miles of progress with Randall. While she was still shy and reserved with him, she was a different girl these days—her attitude softer. The night of the burial she'd come to my room, her eyes reddening with tears. "I've read the letters," she had said, "but then, you knew I would, didn't you? I owe you for that, cousin. And for keeping my letters safe for me. I *can* understand Randall better now. To tell you the truth, I don't think I wanted to face my part of the blame. I had all these high-flown ideas about what my life should be like. Randall must have felt desperate to please me. I don't know. It's all so complicated, but thanks."

She'd looked at me, and I at her, both wishing we knew how to close the gulf between us, and yet each stiff, unsure of the other.

"It was nothing, Charity. I'm glad if I helped."

"You did. You have in more ways than you know. Randall tells me I've done wonders with the children. He credits me with giving them a sense of peace—of being loved. I . . . I think you've had more to do with that these past months than I have."

I didn't like her thinking that. I loved them, yes, but so did she. "Don't say that, Charity."

She lifted her shoulders. "I've forgotten how to play—

165

to have fun. I guess it's just another thing I'll have to add to my list. Goodnight." She went to leave but stopped short of the door. "There is something else, cousin." She sighed. "I wasn't kind to you when Wubbles died. I wanted to hurt you; I don't know why—maybe it was the letters. But none of what I said was true. Will you forgive me?" She'd stood there, her head down and the tears falling like there was no stopping them.

"Oh, Charity." We were suddenly hugging, both of us crying.

"I hope you're listening to me, Lori." Jonas had left the railing and was sitting on the bench next to me. "Because I want you to come. You haven't been the same since Wubbles died. I don't know what it is exactly—you're too quiet, keep to yourself too much. And the kids are right—you don't smile much anymore."

"Oh, of course I smile." I looked up into his eyes to give him evidence.

"That's not the kind of smile I mean. There's no heart in it. What you need is to get away from all this. The mountain is cool and quiet, and the old family home is large. You can have a real rest. Come on, Lady." His hand slipped up under my hair to rest on the nape of my neck. "*Come for me.*"

He was trying to cheer me up, but I wasn't up to new places and conversation with people I didn't know. It would be a strain living in Jonas's half-brother's house, even for three days, and besides, it was too soon. To stay here, to be near where Alex had been, seemed to help. "Jonas—"

"I won't take a no!" His thumb nudged my chin upward. "I hear it coming, but I won't let you refuse. Say yes, girl." The blue eyes glinted a warning. "Yes, Lori Lyn, *yes.*
166 *Say it!*"

But neither did I have the strength to resist this kind of persuasion. Being with Jonas would be wonderful, and we might even find that peculiar friendship we'd shared and then lost. "All right, Jonas. Yes. Maybe that is what I need."

There was a movement behind us. It was Miles. By the

look on his face he wasn't happy, and I wondered how long he'd been standing there. "Evening, Luker."

Jonas shifted closer to me and, surprisingly, his arm dropped about my shoulders. "Evening, Lassiter. How's it going?"

Miles stepped around to face us, his lips tight. "Fine."

"Is it business that's kept you here so long this trip?" Jonas was referring to the fact that Miles hadn't been known to occupy his corner room so long before. He'd always been out more than in, but the situation had reversed in the past weeks.

"Personal business, yes." Miles's gaze shifted to me. "Forgive me, Delores Lyn, but I couldn't help overhearing. Are you sure about this Pine Valley trip? Believe me, it's an exhausting ride—it will take all day, and there's really not that much to do up there. If you need a change, let me take you to San Bernardino. My family's there, and we could show you a much better time."

I glanced at Miles. How dare he belittle Jonas's home like that!

Jonas pushed to his feet. "Well, you've got me, Lassiter. I'm sure that compared to the mountain, there's a lot more going on most anywhere. But it's a rest that the Lady needs—*not excitement.*"

Miles half laughed and in an easy voice that carried only the slightest edge said, "Maybe you should just keep quiet, Luker, and let the lady herself decide what she needs."

"Miles!" I stood. Somehow the discussion was becoming an argument.

"So what is it to be?" Jonas drawled, his lips lifting unpleasantly. His gaze fastened on me, and all his earlier warmth was gone. Only a cold challenge was there. His concern for me seemingly vanished in this flaring contest, and a contest of what? I didn't understand it and didn't like it. I didn't need to have them pulling at me. With my heart giving way, I looked from one man to the other.

"Well?" Jonas pressed. "What do you want, Lady? Tell

us so we'll know." He seemed to be speaking of more than a trip.

"Stop pushing her." Miles sensed how close I was to tears, though the perception had come late.

"Oh, forgive me, Lassiter, but wasn't it *your* idea to let the lady decide, or are you now seeing that maybe I was right to step in after all?"

They'd turned to confront one another, and I started away from them and into the house. Both men called my name, but I kept going until the door of my room was firmly closed and I could be alone.

* * * * *

"*Please go.*" Clarey started in on me the moment I walked into the dark kitchen the next morning. "The children need you there."

"They'll have Jonas, and besides, Clarey, we can't all go off and leave you to run the inn alone."

She was offended. "I ran the inn alone for a great many years before I had Charity or Meg here to help. The three of us will do just fine, and Meg's girls are here. You'll be back on the weekend when we're busiest."

"Clarey, I don't want you working harder because of me."

"I don't plan to. To tell you the truth, Delores, I'm going for an outing with Hal to Dodge's resort tomorrow afternoon. Hal insists *as my doctor* that it's what I need!"

"I agree, but about Pine Valley—"

"Don't be difficult, Delores. *You're going!*"

TWENTY

Less than an hour later the supply wagon was loaded with the trunk Clarey had hurriedly packed for me, the day's food, the wide quilt bed Charity had made for the children's use during the journey, and the jumping children. I found myself aboard the wagon at Jonas's shoulder. It wasn't quite dawn. We were making an early start, Jonas explained, because of the wagon. We'd have to take the long way around, and we'd be lucky to be in Pine Valley by nightfall.

Only moments ago, when I'd asked Jonas to fetch my trunk down the stairs for me, he'd smiled broadly and leaned to whisper, "About last night, well . . ." It was about as close as Jonas could come to an apology. I felt better knowing our trip would not be troubled with ill feelings between us.

Just as the farewells and last-minute instructions were being exchanged, Lyddie Reiley burst out the back door with a small case in her hand and loped toward the wagon crying, "Wait up, wait up. I'm coming too."

Jonas moaned his displeasure, but Clarey was quick to say, "Oh, fine, Lyddie. Jonas will be happy to drop you at Chad's. Is Esther coming too?"

"No, not my sister. Esther's always afraid of imposing,

though I told her with such a fine wagon as this, it's no imposition at all."

The Reiley sisters had a brother who lived and worked at the Chadburn ranch. I at least wasn't sorry she was coming along. She was a notorious talker, and I wouldn't have to worry about making conversation with Jonas for at least half a day.

We waved good-bye as Clarey called out, "Go easy, Jonas. Careful on the steep inclines."

My heart thumped in excitement. *Five days in Jonas's company.*

* * * * *

True to her reputation Lyddie talked—and talked and talked. At first my head spun trying to keep up with her, but soon I adopted Jonas's attitude and let the words fly as I took in the scenery. She rambled on whether we made comments or not.

Not long after leaving St. George, we started up a steep, zigzagging incline. "Jacob's Ladder," the children sang out in back. I hung on tightly, frightened at the sudden ascent. Soon after that we hit patches of heavy sand. Interspersed with Lyddie's tales and sometimes right over them, Jonas pointed out Snow Canyon in the distance and unusual formations that grew out of the rolling landscape like imps or goblins. "A land of confusion," the Lamanites had called the Dixie area, and it truly was. Sweeping mountains to rainbowed plateaus, ghoulish rock structures, valleys and gorges dropping away in unexpected splendor—it was a dizzying country.

We reached Chad's place before noon. Lyddie didn't linger to share our picnic lunch, and we were all glad. We were exhausted—and not just from the ride. The silence sounded so good that even the children respected it.

After resuming our journey, I moved to the back of the wagon with Mara and Aldan. We played games and sang songs until miraculously they both fell asleep at the same

170

time. I went back up to the front seat. Now the quiet was not welcome, but awkward. I hadn't been able to talk freely with Jonas for weeks.

I began a chattery conversation, but Jonas remained unresponsive. I tried asking questions. "Jonas, look at those tracks along the road. What animal made those—rabbits? Deer maybe?"

"Don't know." He'd scarcely looked at them.

I tried again. "What does a ring around the moon mean?"

Jonas turned to me, amused. "How the heck should I know?"

"You're an Indian, aren't you?"

"Am I?"

"Yes. Your mother was half Paiute. Thelma Sackett told me so. That makes you a quarter Indian."

"My grandmother was a full-blooded Paiute, so yes, Lamanite blood runs in my veins. It doesn't necessarily mean I know the Paiute ways. I'm also Danish, but I can't make pastry."

"Oh, Jonas, I think you're mocking me."

He laughed. "Yes, Lady, I am. I'm doing my darndest."

I couldn't resist laughing myself. When Jonas wanted to be pleasant, his down-to-earth, spontaneous charm stole my breath.

"Do you mind my being curious, Jonas?"

"About my parents? No, I'm used to it."

"So tell me about your folks. You know all about my background."

After some determined prodding, he began to talk about his mother.

"She was fourteen, nearly fifteen when she married Sam." 171

"Sam? Your father? You called him Sam?"

"He wasn't much of a father, though he did try in the end. But by then he was Sam, and it stuck. He'd been married before and had three sons—Aaron, Thomas, and

Ross. Ross was about five when Mother went to care for them. She lived with a Mormon family—an elderly couple who had bought Mother from a slave trader when she was a baby. They had her baptized and raised and loved her along with their only daughter, Beth. Whenever possible, Mother hired herself out for domestic work. When Sam Luker's first wife died, he needed household help, and Mother wanted to take the job. But the Spencers wouldn't hear of it—they didn't think it proper for a young girl to be living with a young widower. I guess Sam got desperate and offered to marry her. Mother told me once he would have married anyone to get some help up there and an all-year maid, cook, and caretaker for his children.

"For eight or nine years that was her status—servant. It was a marriage in name only. She lived in a separate part of the house and received no respect from Sam's children. When Sam prospered, he sent his sons off to be educated in the East. With the house empty, I suppose he began looking at my mother for the first time. She was no longer a child, and he fell in love with her. She was lovely. I have a picture, and with it the memory of beauty and softness."

Jonas's voice reflected affection and caring. He'd loved his mother. I felt good knowing that.

"Anyway, I was the result. I was very young when Sam's boys returned home. They were supposedly educated, but not without bias. How they carried on about Mother—especially Ross. I guess Sam was embarrassed or thought he'd betrayed his boys by falling in love with another woman—a half-breed at that. He asked Mother to move back to her old room in the loft and take me with her 'for a time.' Overnight her status reverted back to 'squaw.' How I hated the word! Ross sneered it at me often, and I saw the pain it brought my mother.

"But Mother wouldn't have it—one night she put me on a horse behind her and rode away. Sam caught up with us and forced her back. After that, true to his word, he let the world know that Mother was his wife and that he loved her, and my brothers were made to respect her. We had a pretty good year—just *one* good year. Then she died—a pain in the side, and before Sam could get her off the mountain, she was dead."

No wonder Jonas seldom referred to his childhood. It had been tragic. I knew the emptiness of losing a mother so young. But I'd been blessed with a security Jonas never had.

"What about you, Jonas? With your mother gone, how was it at home for you?"

"Sam tried hard to make it work—and Aaron too. But I never felt a part of them. By then I guess the blame was in me. I was only eight years old—full of resentment. My brothers were years older and full of their own lives. Clarey saw that. Her husband Willis and Sam were in business together in the inn, so Clarey suggested I move in there. It was Clarey who raised me. Willis, Clarey, and Charity were my family. Clarey saw to it that I went to church and to school. She loved me, and she scolded me good when I needed it. And when Sam died, long after I was grown, and left me an equal share of everything he owned, I was almost as shocked as his boys."

"But Jonas, you're Sam's boy, too! Of course he would want you to have an inheritance. He loved your mother, and that means he loved you, too. I'm sure he could see how special you are—how intelligent."

Jonas grinned. "Thanks for the heated defense, honey." His hand covered my own for the briefest of moments. "That was all years ago, and I got through it fine."

"But the Lukers are your people, and if you haven't an affinity for your brothers—"

"Affinity?" He didn't know what I meant.

"You know, a feeling of kinship."

"Aaron and I are close, and I get along with Tom and Ross for the most part. At Christmas, weather permitting, they bring their wives and kids back to the mountain, and sometimes I go too, and we all crowd in the home with

Aaron and his brood. We cut a big, fresh tree. Then we seem almost like a normal family. Someday I'd like you to see it all. I'll talk to Norene, and if we get a mild winter this year maybe we can close up the inn for a few weeks and all of us—Clarey, Charity, Randall, and the kids—could come up for Christmas. Then I'd have *my people* there with me."

I felt as if I would burst. *My people,* Jonas had said. He considered me a part of those he cared for. "Oh, there isn't anything I'd like better, Jonas."

"I consider it a date." His hand grasped mine again. "You won't go running off to Papa or to San Bernardino, will you, Lady?"

"And miss Christmas on the mountain? Not for the world!"

* * * * *

The sun was gone when the wagon creaked up over the final hill. A green valley fell away before us in the dusk, rimmed with a horseshoe of rugged, pine-lush mountains. Involuntarily I gasped. It was so much like my beloved Ashley—pine, aspen, and cottonwood trees, sage and wild grasses, the cool smell, and the sleepy, let-the-world-go-by feel of it all. The homes were quaint and well-built with tidy picket-fenced yards. Brilliant blooms grew alongside the fences and front porches, and everywhere was deep, black soil so rich one could imagine the fragrance of it. And in the center of it all was a temple-white chapel so like my own ward house I found myself getting misty-eyed. I could close my eyes and imagine I was home.

Jonas leaned to inspect my face. "Those can't be tears, girl!"

174   "I'm tired," I defended.

"Hah!" he scoffed. "It's like Ashley, isn't it? That's why I wanted to bring you here."

* * * * *

"We're here!" The children bounded out of the wagon before it had even stopped. I looked at the lighted windows of a lovely, spacious home. It appeared to be red brick with white shutters and trim.

"This was the home you grew up in?"

"Oh, no. Sam built this after Mother's death. I never lived here much." Jonas helped me down from the wagon, his hands lingering on my waist as he set me on the ground.

"Jonas, children?" A woman had come out on the porch. We turned, and Jonas hailed a hello.

Aaron and Norene were older than I expected. They looked remarkably alike, as couples are sometimes prone to do. Their eyes held a matching contentment that spoke of years shared together. I liked them both on sight.

They made me feel at home immediately. Norene called Mara and Aldan back down the stairs. "Of course, you must eat immediately," she said. "We've plenty of hot water, and you can have your baths and get to bed. It's a tiring ride, and don't we know it."

As we moved into the kitchen, Jonas pointed to an oval-framed photograph of Sam Luker and his first wife, Aaron's mother. "That's Camille, and there," he motioned to the fireplace mantel, "is Lena—Mother." Sam looked dark and powerful in a suit and tie. His nostrils flared arrogantly, but the picture was ages old, and the pose might have been more the photographer's doing than Sam's. Camille appeared fragile, but pretty. Lena I liked best, though of course I was prejudiced. But she seemed real, with dark, dark hair arranged in a cloud about a hauntingly lovely face. "When was it painted?"

"Two months before she died."

* * * * *

My bedroom was perfect, white and lavender with lilac wallpaper on the steeply slanted walls and ceiling, and a purple comforter on the bed. Norene had hung my dresses while I bathed, and my other things were placed neatly in drawers. A book lay on my pillow—an anthology of British and American poetry. I was impressed with Norene Luker as a hostess. It was dear of her to think of it, but too tired to

175

read, I moved the book to the dresser, and a yellow envelope tumbled to the floor. It was from Miles.

Delores Lyn, I understand from Clarey that you've decided on Pine Valley. This isn't defeat—only an unavoidable delay. Do rest and enjoy your trip. San Bernardino will wait. The book is for you. Think of me. I shall miss you.

Your Miles

P.S. I've decided to ask for baptism on your return. I trust you will be pleased.

TWENTY-ONE

"Let's get dizzy," Aldan called to his sister. The two jumped from the porch and began whirling about the grass in concentrated gyrations. They begged me to join in.

"Thanks, but Jonas has asked me to go riding. While we're gone, you two take care to mind Norene."

"You don't have to tell us that. Reney lets us do what we want, so we always mind her."

Norene was indulgent, but if any children deserved spoiling, these two did. I found Jonas in the corral. He'd finally come to a decision.

"I'm going to let you have Mae, but go easy. She's frisky and overreacts. I could put a rope on her so I can control her."

I smiled demurely. "If you'd rather, Jonas, I could take your bay."

"No—Jack's excellent, but he's high strung and spooks easily. Here, I'll show you how to mount."

Before he could move, I hooked the stirrup and swung into the saddle. "Where to?"

"I—up toward the canyons, I thought." His confusion was apparent.

Moving my heels to the horse's flanks, I nudged him, and we were off like a shot, circling, then leaping the fence in a graceful movement. Jonas's shout hammered after me, as I knew it would—he even swore, but I didn't stop. I leaned low over the mare's neck and let her take the lead. I wished there were a few more jumps just to make the show all the more spectacular.

All morning long Jonas had been patronizing. "Don't be frightened, Lori. Hold the reins loosely. Don't drop them." I'd taken it all in as a lady should. Over the noon meal a suitable mount—"nothing too spirited"—had been discussed. Norene was worried due to Jonas's concern. She thought we should forget saddle horses and just take the buggy.

"Norene, what we need to do is get this girl out of her cozy carriage and onto a genuine horse—but a safe one!"

I hadn't told Jonas I could ride—but then he hadn't asked. He simply assumed I was inept at every skill he valued. I saw no reason to tell him that Grandmother had insisted I be trained at a riding academy in Denver. I even had clothes designed just for the sport—a riding habit, it was called. It was a jaunty, tailored outfit with a rakish cap. Had I done my own packing, I'd have had it with me.

The road began twisting about, and I reined Mae in to a safer pace. Jonas still had not caught up, so I let Mae take me down to the creek for a leisurely drink. When Jonas still hadn't appeared, we turned and cantered back down the trail. At sight of me, he reined in and waited for me.

"Hi, looking for me?"

His eyes took in my control and obedient mount. "You're good, Lori, all right. But you could have told me!"

It was a mild reprimand. "I could have, but then *you* could have asked if I rode instead of insultingly assuming I couldn't."

"Insulted you, did I?"

I flicked my hair back over one shoulder in a gesture of frustration. "Yes, you did. You're overbearing, Jonas. You insult me all the time."

He cocked a black eyebrow. "All the time?"

"Yes. You assume things about me that aren't at all true,

and I don't like it. Though when it comes down to it, your opinion, *Mr. Luker,* means nothing to me—nothing at all."

He grinned, slid down from his horse, and reached up to pull me from Mae's back all in one graceful, confident motion.

I hesitated, not willing to slide down into his outstretched arms. He intended to kiss me.

"You're a prickly little thing—prickly and pretty." He easily overcame my puny resistance. His head lowered to mine, and his lips parted as they leisurely took mine. I should have refused him, but it had been too long since I'd felt his arms encircling me. I did my best to keep my head and fought a swamping feeling that I feared was love. Our list of differences stretched out limitlessly. And there was Miles . . .

But when his lips left mine, I felt empty, incomplete. We stood a little apart, looking at one another. It was insane for an Ashley to be attracted to such a maverick, yet I was. I sensed a corresponding warring going on in Jonas's thoughts as well, and I was—unreasonably—offended. I dropped my gaze and murmured something about getting on with the ride, but Jonas moved quickly to turn me back to him, crushing me to him, his mouth on the side of my neck.

"Lori, oh, honey, I've missed you."

"Have you, Jonas?"

"Do you think I've liked seeing you on Lassiter's arm every time I turn around?"

"Why haven't you said something? You've been— you've been—"

"Has it just been my fault?"

But there was no time to answer. His mouth covered mine again, and I gave myself up to the mindless, singing joy only this man could inspire. There was only one Jonas in all the world, and while I wasn't sure we got along too well, I knew with all my heart there was no getting along without him either.

The day turned golden. Side by side, sometimes on

179

our horses, and sometimes on foot and hand in hand, we explored the canyons and hills. We came across the scattered debris of hastily built shanties. Jonas explained that it wasn't unusual for fugitives from justice to take refuge in these hills and that his father, Sam, may have been one of them.

"An outlaw? Your father?" My voice cracked, and the word *suitability* flashed before my eyes. I could see Jonas and Papa confronting one another, and I couldn't see how they would ever get on—not in a million years.

"I don't know what Sam did, but he left Texas in a hurry. He was schooled and wealthy, and something happened that he would have been jailed for if he hadn't unloaded his holdings and gotten out. Aaron says whatever it was, Sam did it for good reason, and I think that's probably right. He wasn't one to cheat or take unfair advantage. He joined the Church eventually, and I'm sure whatever it was, he squared it with the Lord."

We rode for a while in silence, then Jonas said, "It bothers you, doesn't it?"

"A little, yes, though I'm not sure why, when I know you. It shouldn't matter that your father got into difficulty, but—"

"I know, I know. It's *your Papa.*" He clamped his lips together tightly and charged ahead on his horse, the wind blowing his hair in all directions.

After a time I caught up with him and was relieved to see that his expression had softened some. "Jonas . . ." He turned. Hunting for some reason for calling out to him, I heard myself asking, "Would you like to go back now?"

"About that story—I don't know why I was so stupid as to tell you something that could easily send you running from me."

I hardly dared let myself believe he could mean it that way, but how else was there to take it? "I'm not running, Jonas."

His head came up. "No?"

"No." I reined in my horse and dropped to the ground. There was a creek ahead.

"Yeah, well maybe you should, Lady." His voice hit at me as he led his own mount to the water.

I was stung. "Jonas, you're confusing me. Are you telling me to run or not?"

"Heck, Lady, we've got problems, don't we? So far, I'm only *sure* that that pretty dude Lassiter isn't the man for you."

"And how is it you know that?"

He grunted. "I just know."

"You don't know Miles worth a darn."

"I know you, and for all your phony attitudes on social standing, Lori, I know you love the gospel and the Church. Lassiter's a gentile through and through. He'll be no help to you or your children spiritually."

"He's changing—he's—" I thought for a moment. "This is confidential, Jonas, so please treat it as such, but Miles plans to ask for baptism. So you don't know as much about him as you think you do!"

"Bah. Baptism doesn't prove anything except that Lassiter is as shrewd in getting himself a pretty wife as he is in running his sheep business. He knows he's got to be a member to get you, so he becomes a member."

"You're wrong!"

"I'm not."

"I don't want to talk about it."

"That's fine with me. Just remember what I've said and don't go promising him anything. I'd hate to have to bust his head in for getting in my way."

"Jonas!" I laughed at the mock violence in his words knowing that he'd be far more likely to walk away than fight for me. Still, it was a heady thought having Jonas and Miles slinging it out over me. "But I admit I like your candor."

"Yeah? And there's lots more you like about me, isn't there!" He was unashamedly fishing, but I didn't mind.

"Oh, lots and lots more."

"Like what?"

"Jonas," I scolded, embarrassed. "It's getting late—"

"Tell me. What is it you like specifically?"

I met his eyes. "Everything—just about."

"*Just about?*" He growled his disappointment, then grinned. And what a grin it was—his teeth and blue eyes flashing, the rough-hewn clefts lining his proud jaw. I loved him! All right, yes I did! I loved his indomitable spirit, his independent soul. Whatever our differences, where it counted we thought alike. Jonas and I—Lori Luker. It sounded as natural as breathing. *Lori Luker.* I had to be his, and I ached to tell him. But it was a man's place to speak of these things first, so I, with heart overflowing, held my silence.

* * * * *

"You'll find writing paper in the left-hand drawer," Norene instructed as I sat down at her secretary to write to Papa and my sisters. I wanted to tell them about the magic of the valley before leaving it.

I moved a few letters in my search for the paper, and my name flashed before my eyes. I picked up a rather dog-eared piece of stationery. Had Mara or Aldan written this? My eyes skipped over the poorly formed, misspelled words to the name beneath. Jonas—it was from Jonas.

I shut the drawer wishing I hadn't seen it. Jonas wasn't precise in his grammar, but he certainly expressed himself well. I was certain that he'd had more education than the awkward letter implied. Anyway, *what did it matter?* So what if he couldn't spell properly. I loved him. And what did penmanship and spelling have to do with human kindness and decency and manliness?

182

But I sat for a long while staring through the window at the empty sky outside.

TWENTY-TWO

Our first day back at the inn was a busy one. It was also my twenty-third birthday, and Clarey had spread the word. Everyone had slipped into the kitchen at one time or another to wish me well. Miles told me he had a little remembrance to deliver later when I could spare him a moment. The children announced a family party at four and that I was not to go into Mara's bedroom or look in her doll cupboard under any circumstances!

"Make a solemn promise on your life!" Mara said.

"The best surprise is the dance and barbecue. After cake we're all going in Dr. Hal's surrey to Washington," Aldan added.

"You're telling! Grandma said we weren't to tell yet."

Aldan clapped a hand over his mouth.

"I won't tell a soul, Aldan. In fact, with all I've got to do today, I'm sure to have forgotten all about it by four."

"Can you do that?"

"Do what?" I turned a blank expression on him. "What *are* you talking about?"

Sometime around two I missed Old Dog. I called him several times throughout the morning, but he hadn't responded. He'd lost most of his wanderlust since Alex's death—perhaps he had gone back to exploring again. But by midafternoon when he still hadn't come around to eat, I sent the children searching along the back canal and the orchards. Miles came out, and I asked him to help, too.

"Hasn't Meg Gibbons told you?"

"Told me what?"

He rubbed his hands together nervously. "I'd rather not have to do this, Delores Lyn—I know you loved that mongrel."

Something had happened—Miles was using the past tense. "Has he run away, Miles?"

"No, my dear, it's much more final than that."

So Old Dog was dead.

Miles tried to comfort me, though his matter-of-fact tone was more irritating than comforting. "The dog was ancient. He's been a nuisance since I first came here. Until you took a liking to him, I wanted him disposed of."

"He wasn't a nuisance to me."

"No, of course he wasn't. That was tactless of me. Forgive me."

"How did it happen?"

"He just wandered off. Dr. Hallum spotted the carcass along the river road two days ago. I'm sure he simply died of old age. Now forget all that!" Miles motioned for me to come with him. "I've been waiting all day to give you your birthday present. Let's sit here in the arbor where we'll have some privacy."

I did as he asked and was presented with a tiny green velvet box. As I opened it, Miles watched, his eyes glittering expectantly . . .

* * * * *

184   I tried not to dwell on Old Dog. It wasn't fair to those who were trying to make my birthday such a nice day. But beneath the laughter and happy wishes, I felt an inescapable strain of sadness. Had he gone off looking for me? I found it hard to shake the sense of loss and the conviction that had I stayed home from the mountain the poor creature would still be alive.

At three-thirty Clarey sent me up to change for the party with instructions to report back to the parlor at four. I washed, redid my hair, and slipped on a white eyelet dress. The emerald brooch that had been Miles's gift was clipped at my throat. It lent the only color, and I thought the effect was striking.

Charity had made my birthday cake herself—a three-tiered wonder decorated with swirls of pink frosting and crushed peppermints. I was touched that she had taken such pains for me. Her gift was a white-beaded purse, presented with a hug! The children gave me a button bracelet in a rainbow of colors, and I promptly put it on. Clarey's gift was a glamorous silvery green shawl that caused me to gasp in delight.

"So, Lady, which hand do you take?" Jonas had waited until last, both hands hid behind his back, and I supposed he held a package in them.

"That one." I grinned, pointing to the left.

He brought the hand out, palm up—empty. "Nope." He waited for me to choose the other hand.

"All right, then that one."

But again his hand was empty. "Wrong again. Guess outside on the front porch."

"Outside on the front porch?"

"Nope!" He pumped his brows with pleasure. "Guess out back beneath an overturned bushel basket—"

"Jonas—" Clarey began to scold.

"Shhh. Let her guess."

I humored him. After all, it was my birthday. I could afford to. "Out back . . ."

"Beneath an overturned bushel basket," he prompted.

"Beneath an overturned bushel basket."

"Right!"

The children bolted ahead of me through the door. "Hey, you two, wait up!" But by the time the little group had reassembled in the back yard the basket was rolling in the dust and as empty as Jonas's hands had been.

"Oh, Jonas!" Everyone chorused together, wearying of his game.

"Well, that's where I put it." A sudden whimpering and scratching turned our eyes back to the house. There, scarring up the doors as effectively as his predecessor, was a tiny, rust-colored puppy. No one needed to tell me who his papa was!

* * * * *

The ride to Washington in Dr. Hal's primitive though roomy surrey was made all the more fun by the fact that we were only one of a long caravan of carriages, wagons, and other rigs going to the same party. It was a political rally, really, Clarey had explained, but the talk would be short and the food and dancing plentiful. Mara (sitting in back with Jonas and me) and Aldan (up front with Clarey and Hal) were ecstatic that they had been invited to come along, though Charity had informed them that after the barbecue they were going to Lorana's to be tended and put to bed. But even this knowledge didn't curtail their enthusiasm. They bounced about, pulling faces and waving at their parents, Randall and Charity, riding in the buggy behind, and talked a steady stream.

"Will we have beef and beans like last time?"

"Can we stay and listen to Mr. Stahlei's band just a little while?"

"Are Lorana's kids coming too?"

Weary of the questions, Clarey suggested we sing, and sing we did, Jonas's arm slipping around my shoulder. I settled back against his arm and smiled into his eyes. He smiled back, then stiffened as he spotted the emerald brooch. "New, or part of the family jewels?"

"New—a birthday present."

It wasn't what he wanted to hear. "From old Miles, right?"

Puzzled at his reaction at first, I then began to understand. He was comparing his gift of the puppy to Miles's extravagance.

186

"Jonas, don't! I love Rusty. He's what I needed more than anything."

"Do you think you should keep that pin? It's pretty expensive, I'd say, and wearing it suggests an attachment to Lassiter, doesn't it?"

Mara had overheard. "Are you going to marry him, Lori? Are you?"

"It's a birthday present, nothing more."

"But are you going to marry Mr. Lassiter, Lori?" Mara wouldn't be put off.

The silence was strained as everyone waited for my answer. "I—I don't think so."

"You don't sound too sure," Jonas muttered into my hair, but he kept his arm around me.

* * * * *

"Still the belle of the ball!" Jonas said as he cut in. We had danced once at the beginning, but not since. He was a beautiful dancer, and I had been disappointed he hadn't cut in earlier.

"I've missed you," I whispered as he whirled me into a shadowy corner of the hall. "Where've you been?"

"Outside. Mel, Debra, and Melissa are here, did you know?"

"No, but that's wonderful—"

"Yeah, wonderful. Now you can show off your fancy birthday brooch—"

"Jonas," I began, but he didn't give me a chance to object to his taunting.

"What do you say, Lady, shall we stop wasting time and get married, you and I?"

Stunned, I could only stare at him. 187

"You heard right, girl." He was wearing a smile, but I didn't like his angry tone. If this was a proposal of marriage, then it was all wrong.

"Jonas, what are you saying? Do you want to marry me?"

His lids lowered. "I guess that depends on you."

Offended at his brutal handling of what was to me the dearest subject in all the world, I tried to match his glib manner, "Oh?"

"Do you want to marry me, Lori? Yes or no?"

"Jonas, don't!" It wasn't the proposal I'd been waiting to hear—that I'd dreamed of. He hadn't even mentioned love. I couldn't help thinking of his argument with Miles over my going to Pine Valley. Was this another contest of wills, or was his pride hurt because of Miles's gift?

"Don't what? Don't ask you to marry me? Are you saying no?"

"I'm asking you not to do it this way."

"What's that supposed to mean? I'm asking you to marry me. Do you want to or not?" His temper was beginning to flare.

"Now just a minute, Jonas. Let me think."

"But haven't you already? I can see in your eyes that you're attracted to me. In fact, Lori, you can't stay away. But I'm not the kind of man you've always planned on marrying, am I? Not much formal education—can't write or spell decently, and I live in a wasteland of a place—at least in your eyes I do, and I've Lamanite blood running in my veins, though that perhaps could be forgiven if I were rich and powerful. But alas, I'm not, and not likely ever to be. Sums it up, don't you think?"

It was true, everything he'd said—at least that's how I had seen it at one time—*not now.* I loved him, and my former concerns seemed shallow and unimportant. They'd belonged to a different girl in a different life.

"But then, you aren't the girl of my dreams either."

I'd been staring at his shirt front, but my head went up at that, and I just caught myself from tripping over his shoes as he suddenly stopped dancing and stood stock still. "No, you're too sophisticated for a man ever to be sure what's real about you and what isn't. You're materially minded, and that's always getting in the way of your softer nature. You don't know your place as a woman. You'd be a hard wife to handle—too beautiful and too spirited. And to top it off, what wifely skills and inclinations do you have? If the food we ate a while back is anything to judge by . . . So you see, Lady, if I'm short-changing you, then you are doing the same thing to me!"

"But Jonas, if that's how you really feel, then why even ask?"

"Because . . ." He drew the hand he'd been holding to his mouth and kissed it. "I want you to be mine, and I think if we worked at it we could both make something of the other. So what's your verdict, Lady? Do we tie the knot or don't we?"

Was that a vulnerable look in his eyes? Had a little warmth crept into his voice, or was it all my wishful thinking? He hadn't said he loved me, but then maybe it wasn't necessary. *Jonas loved me.* It might be unspoken, but I could feel his love, and what a joy to be his, to lie each night in his strong arms, to bear his children and work at his side for the rest of our lives.

"So, I have your answer." He let me go.

"But I haven't said a thing, Jonas."

"You don't have to, honey. Your big green eyes say it all. You've run up the score and I'm sadly lacking. Not good enough for the Lady Delores and her high-and-mighty family. Let's just forget I asked." He was turning away. I caught at his sleeve.

"Jonas, wait a minute. Let me say something!"

"Don't look so defeated, Lori. Lassiter's rich and educated. Maybe you can get him to pop the question."

"He already has."

"Then that explains your silence. You've already said yes to him, I take it—"

"Will you listen, Jonas? I turned Miles down cold. I refused him, do you hear? Today—this afternoon—when he gave me the pin, there was also a ring, and I said no. He told me to take the brooch to remember him by. I didn't want it, but he is a friend, Jonas. He wanted me to have it for my

189

birthday. The pin is a gift from a friend—nothing more."

But he wasn't listening. He'd been searching the whirling crowd, and as his eyes lit up, I saw the reason.

"Melissa? Where the devil have you been all night? Excuse me, pal." He placed a heavy hand on her companion's shoulder. "This is my girl, Ives, remember?"

I don't remember much about the rest of the dance. I remember only that I laughed a lot and danced my feet to blisters. My childhood hadn't been as useless as some led me to believe. No, I'd been taught thoroughly how to camouflage all chinks in my armor—how above all to maintain poise, dignity, and self-respect. So with flags flying I played the part of the spoiled, rotten Delores Lyn that Jonas so despised. I flirted with a vengeance and, ignoring the fact that Jonas chose to dance the rest of the evening with Melissa only, succeeded in having seven different fellows offer me a ride home. I accepted Michael Cotter, a young elder who'd once been the speaker in Clarey's ward. He, I knew, was a gentleman, and in the midst of a howling polka, we slipped out the door into the night.

Only Debra and Mel had seen us go, and I asked them to convey the message to Clarey and Hal so that no one need worry on my account. After I'd done that, I wondered why I'd bothered. Delores Lyn Ashley didn't care about the inconveniences of others—no, she was a self-centered little nobody who did as she pleased and let the rest of the world go hang.

* * * * *

I slept in until eight-thirty the next morning. When I awoke the sun was shining boldly into my room. I woke up with a start, fighting the black staggers. Why had I been allowed to oversleep? I dressed hurriedly and rushed down the back stairs.

"What are you doing up already?"

Was she jibing me? "Morning, Meg. Sorry I wasn't here for the breakfast work. Has everyone finished?"

190

"Jonas told us all to let you have some sleep. He said you'd had a bad night and not to disturb you."

How had Jonas known I'd lain awake until the dawn hours? I'd muffled my tears in my pillow and hadn't lit the lamp.

"You do look ragged, Miss. Go on and try to catch some more—"

"I'm fine! I don't know what Jonas said, but I never felt better, and I slept like a log last night. You should have been pounding my door down. It's a beautiful day—it's cooler, don't you think?"

With a grinding headache I attended Sunday School with Miles. It was well worth the effort, because as I sat there listening to our teacher talk about the importance of prayer in our lives, I realized Jonas had been right about one thing. Miles wasn't converted. He was going through the motions all right, nodding his head appropriately and even squeezing my hand on occasion to indicate a rush of spirit, but following the meeting as we walked out into the autumn sunlight, I put the question to him.

"Do you believe it, Miles? Any of it? Do you pray?"

His eyes searched mine, but he didn't answer.

"Miles, I was honest about my feelings for you. Please have the courtesy to be honest with me about this. It means so much."

"I have been hoping that you would come to love me and that I would come to love your church." He took my hand in his, patting it in an affectionate way. "But no, my dear girl, I don't. But you, with your sweet faith, you make me want to. Perhaps someday I will."

The rest of the day was a nightmare. I felt wretched, but committed to my stand of jovial light-heartedness, I played my role to a T. I sang at Clarey's piano with Miles and sat with the Reiley sisters as they rocked in the parlor listening as the Edison scratched out their favorite songs. I gave audience to Lyddie as she recited the oft-told story of her Uncle Lon herding sheep on Buckskin Mountain.

191

As far as I could tell, Jonas hadn't been home all day, but then, I wasn't taking chances. During Sunday School he'd sat up front with the Stubbs family, his arm conspicuously around Melissa. I expected him to repeat the same thing at sacrament meeting, but he wasn't there. I could have screamed, for my head was coming apart and I longed for some sleep. Had I known he wasn't attending, I could have remained at home and not bothered trying to keep my chin so conspicuously up.

"It's happening," Clarey had confided as we walked home after church. She was ecstatic that Randall and Charity were working things out. They had taken the children and gone to their former ward for services. "Randall's wooing her back. I knew it was still there for my little girl, and I'm so relieved—so grateful it's all working out at last."

"I am too, Clarey. Charity is so dear."

"Oh, isn't she! And so is Randall. You like him, don't you?"

I did and told her so, and Clarey spent the rest of the trek home telling me about the little house they'd decided on buying. "It's just perfect, Delores—only two houses away from Hal's."

"Really? And why is it important she be close to Dr. Hallum, Clarey?"

But she answered only with the most girlish giggle I'd ever heard coming from this cousin, and I knew the recent lights in her eyes weren't only from happiness for her daughter's future but for her own as well. The widow Clarey Casston was in love again!

For three full days Jonas stayed away. "He's trying to help Mel get his house done before cold weather hits." Clarey brushed my concerns aside with the wave of her hand. "He hasn't been there much this summer, you know."

She believed that, but I felt sure it had a lot more to do with Melissa Stubbs. He wanted to hurt me and he was succeeding.

Wednesday evening when he rode in I met him behind the house. "Could we talk a minute, Jonas?"

He rubbed at the whiskers on his face. "Yes. All right, let's talk."

We moved to the grape arbor. The sun was setting, and for the first time since my arrival, the air was uncomfortably chilly. I didn't know how to start—especially when Jonas was sitting so far away and taking such pains to not so much as look at me.

"So?" He urged, and then slapped at his knees as if impatient to be somewhere else.

"Jonas, did you really mean that proposal of marriage?" *Silence.* It was a bad start. Why had I put it like that?

"Oh, Jonas, please. I love you. And I want to marry you, I do! You caught me off balance at the dance, but I should have told you then, and I would have in the end if you hadn't lost your temper with me."

Still Jonas kept his distance and his cruel silence, his eyes studying the toe of his boot while I waited and prayed. Would nothing soften that hard profile? "Jonas, *say something.*"

"Look, honey, I'm sorry if I've hurt you." His voice was strangely hoarse. "But I've done a lot of thinking about this, and it wouldn't work anyway."

"That's ridiculous—"

"Lori, listen to what I have to say. It isn't easy."

The tone of his voice sounded a death knell inside me. He couldn't mean this—not really.

"My mother and Sam tried it—two people, poles apart, and it was a disaster. I don't want that for us or for our kids."

"But we're not poles apart. I've changed, Jonas—grown toward you. What used to matter just doesn't anymore. I've got hold of real values, Jonas, and money and position and all the other things you threw in my face at the dance, they're just . . . just substitutions for happiness. Grandmother cherished them, and so I thought I did too, but—"

193

"You're beautiful, honey. You were made for beautiful things. After our marriage, you'd long for what I could never give you—"

"Stop it! Be fair—"

"Lady, before you say anything more, you'd better know I'm engaged to Melissa. We're getting married next month. It's been a long time coming, and it's right. Melissa knows this life—loves it here. We're a lot alike."

Somehow I got to my feet. It just wasn't possible he'd done this. He loved me—*me!* I must have said it aloud, for Jonas shook his head and reached for my hand.

"Lori, I'm attracted to you as much as you are to me—"

"*Attracted!*" It was a weak word.

"But I've never said I loved you, have I?"

"But you do. I know you do! Be honest, Jonas. *You do!*" It couldn't be happening—Jonas throwing me over, telling me it was all a mistake and that he didn't love me at all but had only been attracted to me as if I were a soulless piece of furniture in a shop window.

"Of course I care about you, Lori. I always will. You're something special, believe me."

"Please! Don't be kind to me. You've said enough." It had been my voice making those funny sobbing sounds. The tortured words had been my words, and Jonas looked at me as if I'd run a knife through him.

"Oh, Lori—"

I couldn't stay there. That was my only conscious thought. I couldn't stay there and be near him another minute.

"Lori, come back! Where are you going?"

I ran blindly, mindlessly. I was in the street. Horses coming fast upon me shied, and shouts echoed through my head. The thud of feet came up behind me, or perhaps the pounding was my dying heart, bursting with pain in my chest. A horse was tied off in the shadows, a small, beautiful roan. She was like Ruby, Papa's favorite. I crossed and, reaching up for the saddle horn, swung onto her back. We were off and running into the night, Ruby and I.

TWENTY-THREE

My back and legs hurt, but my head hurt most of all. It was spinning, and I couldn't get my eyes to focus. I sat up. Where was I? In the road? Yes, I'd been thrown. I hadn't gone a mile and I'd been thrown. There'd been a near accident, a child. Ruby had reared back.

"That you, sweetie?" I smelled alcohol as the face thrust its way into my vision. "I thought so. Here, I'll help ya up. You lean on ol' Con till yer feelin' yerself."

"Mr. Trouseman?" I closed my eyes.

"Just a nasty fall." He sucked in a breath, the corners of his mouth wet. "No need to go all panicky!"

"Con, thanks, but I'll take her home." It was Jonas. He was sliding from a horse above us, reaching down for me.

"No! Please, Mr. Trouseman." I pushed back into Con's arms. "Would *you* take me home?"

"Sure thing." He was laughing now, his hands closing around my waist. "Sorry, Luker, I've kept my distance like you tol' me, but you heard it yerself. The Lady prefers me. C'mon, little miss, I've got my wagon right here."

"Lori, don't be foolish." Jonas was blocking our way. "Let me take you back to the inn. You're hurt."

There was no need to refuse him a second time, for Connan Trouseman was half carrying, half pushing me toward his wagon.

Jonas followed behind, and not until I was walking up the path to the inn with Con's arm supporting me did I lose consciousness.

* * * * *

"Concussion, no doubt," Dr. Hal diagnosed late that night. "You see the difference in her pupil size? She'll have to stay down—I mean complete bed rest until she heals."

I wasn't certain how long I stayed there in Mara's room. But when I awoke with a clear head, it was night again, and I was alone. I wanted to tell Clarey about my leaving, but I knew it was no good.

I tiptoed up the dark stairs to my room and packed a small bag. Of course, I'd need more clothes for the long trip home, but I could purchase them on the way. If I delayed, they'd stop me, and too much had happened too fast for me to stay another minute. Besides, my usefulness here was at an end. Clarey was well and on her feet and likely to marry Hal soon. Charity would in a week's time be moving out with the children to her new home with Randall. Debra had made her own life as she should with her husband. Alex and Old Dog were dead, and now Jonas . . . Jonas was gone too.

I scribbled a note of explanation and kissed the children good-bye as they slept. With the ticket Charity had purchased for me long months ago tucked in my hand, I let myself out into the night.

Surprisingly, it wasn't night at all but approaching dawn, I realized as I reached the depot. A freighter wagon was leaving for Milford, and if I would settle for a seat next to the driver, I had only a ten-minute wait.

196

* * * * *

The rig, stacked high with an odd assortment of boxes, barrels, and crates, slogged up the countless hills and clattered down them again, the squat driver at my shoulder as silent as the gray and sunless day.

We'd had rain since starting out again from Summit, slow, drizzling rain in a hazy fog that turned the empty country we were hurrying through into a muted, darker extension of the low sky, making it fuzzy and unreal in a way that made me wonder if I'd ever seen any of this country before, though of course I had from the rocking window of the old Concord that Melvin Stubbs had hired for Debra and me on our trip down. That other sunhot journey seemed years ago, and the troubles I'd then carried heavy in my heart now appeared so mild that I marveled I'd ever been so frivolous. My whole focus had been my disturbed position in Ashley society and Papa's condemnation. I smiled through the mist in my eyes to the misty miles that sprawled in all directions of the lone wagon, and I pushed at the funny knot of pain lingering behind my brow.

Seemingly unrelated decisions one after another had brought me here, and my coming had forced a confrontation with myself. I was in truth a better person than I'd known, but then that might be true of everyone. Anyway, it was something—small consolation at this moment maybe, but something to hold to. I needn't keep thinking I'd found what I'd wanted most only to lose it completely. I'd been given much I could keep.

I hadn't thought out my destination yet. There hadn't been time, and now, with nothing ahead but time, the decision seemed unimportant. I'd go where I'd go—north probably . . . somewhere north. Vacuously untroubled by my uncharted future, the only firm certainty seemed my decision not to go home. I was twenty-three years old, grown up, grown away.

Home was the past—Grandmother and foolish bright days of parties and new wardrobes and young awkward beaux. It meant Sundays on the open porch with my beautiful sisters—irridescent lives that I knew now were superficial. Papa had watched, half approving, half disapproving, indecisive about his house of females. Had he longed for the boys he didn't have, for the wife who had died? I didn't know my father. It was a shame. I judged him and he judged me and yet, neither of us knew the other at all.

I wiped at my eyes and swallowed the thickness in my throat. I glanced at the driver, wishing he'd talk so I needn't keep thinking and thinking.

"Do you still think we'll make Milford today?"

"Have to. These supplies are promised in Frisco in the morning."

"And we'll arrive by what time?"

"The rain's not helping." He hahed at the teams, then reached down into the boot for a strip of dried beef. It was smelly, and I felt a rush of nausea as the odor hit my nostrils. I'd been queasy all along, drowsy to the point of stupor, and my head ached.

That afternoon we came to a settlement and changed teams again. I was given a piece of bread and meat, which I gladly ate, but I wasn't allowed to rest a minute. My head spun with a fog more real than the surrounding mist. I was lifted up onto my seat, and we clattered back onto the road again. My clothes were damp through, and I felt chilled. I tried to keep my mind on the train. Once I'd boarded, I could sleep . . .

Sheep laughed at us and children raced alongside the wagon as we pulled into another station. I remembered it— a German couple there had fixed us soup and chatted while Mel and Willis had fixed a broken wheel on our trip down.

I didn't understand that I was being left until it had happened. I heard the knocking of crates and the rattling of wheels as I sat at the table inside. He'd hardly had time to water the teams. I moved to the door and caught a glimpse of the driver hunched over the reins, the wagon slamming
out of the yard.

I turned back to the table and caught sight of my brown case. So he'd meant to dump me here!

The door closed, and the woman I remembered came in from the garden. She was large-boned and round-faced, her hair done up in braids about her ears. She placed a basket of squash on the sideboard.

"Mackey's carrying payroll, I bet. Makes him nervous."

"But I've paid him to take me to Milford. We're still a few hours off, aren't we?"

"About two is all. He said you've been acting strange—that you bob about on the wagon like you might fall off. He was worried, fraulein."

"*Me strange?* We've been driving for hours, and he hasn't said ten words."

"That's Mackey. His life is freighting. You eat, rest. You catch another tomorrow—maybe a coach or a carriage."

* * * * *

"Wach auf, meine kleine freundin, wake up."

Why couldn't they let me sleep just a little. Couldn't Charity see I couldn't get enough sleep? It had certainly turned cold—cold! Abominable weather, this St. George, going from one extreme to another.

My eyes traveled over dim log walls. My clothes were heaped on a battered bench in the corner. I wasn't at Cottonstreet at all. Of course not—I didn't belong there anymore. The realization swept through with the force of a physical pain.

"Ist es dir gut?" The door opened, and the German woman peeked into the room. "Are you all right, fraulein? You sleep and sleep. Two wagons and a buggy you miss."

"I'm sorry, I'll get up now." I shuffled about the chilled room, washing and dressing in bungling disorientation. What *was* the matter with me? Maybe that fall I took. After I'd boarded the train, I could stop over at some little place and rent a room and rest until I felt more myself.

My dark blue traveling dress felt damp and was terribly wrinkled, but I had no choice but to put it on. The only other I'd brought with me I wanted to save for job hunting. My hair was impossible to handle. The rain had tightened the curls, and they'd sprung awry in all directions. I brushed through it and secured it in a clumsy bun. I tried again, but with no greater success. I looked awful—gray, frumpy, wrong.

I yanked out the pins and started over. The results were even worse. Grietje, the German woman, stared at me from across the room.

"I braid your hair, ja?"

"Thanks, but I'll redo it later. It needs washing, I think."

A canvased wagon moved into the yard. "That'll be Poe."

I asked if he might provide a ride to the train. "Ja, Poe will take you, but he makes many stops and will make you wait. You wait for something else."

But Mr. Poe was more than happy to take me straight in to Milford after I'd paid him two dollars—half the price of the train fare to Salt Lake City.

It was late afternoon when Mr. Poe dropped me opposite the depot. I stared for a time at his diminishing wagon and then at the windows of the train depot. The street was crowded with buckboards and horses, but not another woman was in sight, and I felt conspicuous and out of place. Where was I to go—Cache Valley? Idaho? Nevada? *Where?*

I lugged my case with me across the street to the ticket office, all too aware of my travel-worn appearance. I glanced skyward with a sigh. It was growing dark again, would be raining soon by the feel of it. It had been a long time since I'd seen the sun—three days—longer. I'd left it a century ago back in St. George with Jonas.

The wind came up, billowing my heavy skirts, whining down the street, and rising to chatter in the old, yellowing trees. I was cold. According to Mr. Poe, I had a while to wait before a northbound train came through, but it couldn't hurt to get my ticket and stow my case. Then perhaps I'd find a shop and purchase a clean dress and a warm coat.

My stomach rumbled as I smelled the delicious aroma of hot bread. Yes, I'd take time to eat, too. A full stomach would lift my spirits.

"Where to, miss?" The young agent licked his fingers and smacked his lips as I looked longingly at the half-eaten slice of bread in his hand.

"Is there a bakery close?"

He laughed. "Nah, this is Ma's. But you could eat at the hotel across the way. Mabel will take care of you." He made a sound then that drew my eyes to his. His gaze was rounded into a great stare. But he didn't know me—I'd never seen him before in my life. Surely, even with my hair and soiled dress, I couldn't look as bad as all that.

"Something wrong?" I shifted and glanced behind me, thinking perhaps his reaction had been for someone else.

"No! No!" He answered quickly, then turned and disappeared into a room at the back.

I turned my attention to the timetable hanging high on the wall. I could go on toward Frisco, a rough mining town, and from there to Caliente, Nevada, the end of the line, or I could backtrack toward home—Leamington, Juab, Nephi, Payson, Spanish Fork. I'd ridden through them, and their names were at least familiar. I settled on Nephi. If job prospects weren't good there, I could always go on to Provo.

It was a relief having at last decided something, and the fuzziness seemed to recede now that I had something to put my mind to. With some impatience, I looked for the ticket agent's return. When the door finally opened, I found my eyes locked with those of Jonas Luker.

"Ain't that her? Your description fits. Red hair, pretty?" The agent moved out from behind him, a self-satisfied smile spreading across his face.

TWENTY-FOUR

I didn't know what to do. I was trapped. I whirled, searching for a place to run, but I stumbled over my case and sent it slamming to the boardwalk. I tried to right it again, but it wouldn't stay put and fell hard onto my toe. I jumped at the pain, tears starting.

"You seem surprised to see me." Jonas's tone was dry, unkind.

"Yes, I am surprised."

"Oh, why is that?" The question was terse, clipped. He was angry—deeply angry. "You *knew* I'd follow you."

"I didn't think—"

"Oh, yes, you did. How could I leave it like that? *How?* After that fall, you were stunned, hurt, and needing help, and who did you turn to? To the man you'd just claimed to love so much—wanted to marry? No!" His lips came together over his teeth. "You'd rather accept help from Trouseman—go into his loathsome arms than come near me."

"Jonas—" It just wasn't possible he didn't understand.

"And then after Hal had explained that you had a concussion and needed to stay in bed, you go gallivanting off across the country—that very night! Your injury could have been serious. Maybe it still is, and do you say a word—

one word—to any of us? Did you really expect I wouldn't come racing after you?"

His accusations encountered silence. After all the hurt he had given me in the last week, I couldn't believe he was still prepared to give me more.

"Answer me, girl. What did you expect—" He bit off an expletive, but too late. I closed my eyes against his anger and picked up my case. The hotel. I'd go across and get a room. If I missed one train, there'd be another.

The streets were emptying out now, and the wind settling. Thunder snarled across the land, and I felt the first of the rain hard against my face.

"Lori, wait." He was trying to take my case from me.

"Go away."

"I lost my temper. I *shouldn't* have, but I've been worried out of my skull, honey. It wasn't what I'd planned, yelling at you—not even remotely. I—I was going to be on my best behavior—handle this like a gentleman you could admire, but—*Lori, listen, will you?*" His hand came out and he stopped me. "I've been waiting here for days, and I'd begun to think something had happened to you or you'd slipped by me. You understand how it is, don't you? And then I saw you standing at the window looking lost and ill, and *for what?*" He brought me around to face him, his features imploring me to forgive his earlier harshness.

It didn't make any sense his being here. He was going to marry Melissa, so what was he doing coming after *me?* Didn't he know this didn't help either of us?

He reached again to take my case. Stubbornly I backed away, and giving up, he stuffed his hands into his pockets. "Can't you see I wanted to wring that little neck of yours for what you've put me through?"

The rain was coming in a downpour now, and both of us were getting wet to the skin. One of us should have moved, but we stood stock still in the middle of the road, my fingers locked over the handle of the suitcase, and Jonas grimacing up at the sky and then down at me.

203

"There's trouble up the line—a train derailed or something. They're not sure, but I kept thinking if you're on that train, hurt, I'd never forgive myself."

"You shouldn't have worried. I'm fine."

"You don't look it. You look done in—rougher than I've ever seen you."

"Thank you very much."

His lips tightened at that. "You're shivering. You didn't even stop to take a coat. I know—Clarey checked through your things. I brought that fur thing. Come on, let's get out of this." He made another try at my case. It was childish to continue to fight him for it, so I let it go. With his hand under my elbow, he propelled me across the last few yards and up under the covered porch of the hotel. "We'll get a couple of rooms so you can recuperate some before coming back to St. George."

I suddenly understood. This was another rescue mission! It had been an assignment from Clarey, yes. Jonas was often sent out on rescue missions; didn't I know that? He'd come after me twice before—once at the shivaree party and again after the sandstorm, and all at Clarey's instigation. This was part of his Family Responsibility, as he saw it. I was to return, to resume my stay at the inn, go back to work there and eventually be forced to witness Jonas's marriage.

"I'm not going back."

He nodded as if he'd expected me to protest. "Be honest, Lori. You didn't want to love Dixie, but you do—you don't really want to go home anymore. I know that, and I also know you're in rotten shape. You can't take on a long train ride right now."

I looked away from those disturbing eyes and stepped to the edge of the dripping porch, my gaze on the white depot squatting under the dismal fog of rain. "But I'm not going home. I . . . I thought I'd get off at Nephi for now. I could be there in a few hours. Then I *will* get a room and rest up until I'm completely better. I'm not stupid, Jonas." I understood their worry, understood why Clarey and Debra and everyone needed to know I'd got on my way safely and that my plans were sound and reasonably thought out. Well, now they could be reassured and Jonas had done his duty. We could say good-bye quickly and be done with it. My composure was slipping. I couldn't continue talking to him—I just *couldn't.*

"Lori, be reasonable. We don't need to start back right away, but you've got to face up to things. There's so much I want to say. I've hurt you and—"

"No . . . no."

"It was unforgivable, but I was doing what I thought I had to—"

"*No, Jonas!* Not again. Don't talk about it—just go. I'm fine, and I'll stay fine, I promise I will." I knew I should put out a hand of farewell—something. "Tell everyone I'll write."

"Lori, I can't let you go off to Nephi!" The case dropped behind him and he came toward me.

Disregarding the storm, I flew down the steps. "You haven't any say in the matter, Jonas—"

"Oh, yes I do! With you I'll *always* have a say, and you know it."

The nerve of the man! I was halfway across the muddy street, but before I could make my escape altogether, he had me and was dragging me back under the shelter.

I struggled against him. Was I to be left with no pride at all? "I want to get my ticket, and right now—"

"I told you there aren't any more trains today, not going north anyway. They've got trouble—"

"It doesn't matter." I refused to be boxed in. "I'll go on to Frisco." I tried again for the street.

He gave me a rough shake. "Would you settle down? That mining town would eat a little girl like you alive. You're coming home with me!"

"I won't." But there was no getting past him, no shaking off his iron grip. I broke then, crying uncontrollably. How could he do this to me—I'd already begged him to take me as his wife and he'd refused. Was the hurt and humiliation never to end? What? Did he need to witness it all over again?

"Don't, honey. I've bungled everything, I know." I was in his arms. I tried to push away, but he held me tight, held me with my head against his chest as I wept. The anger was gone, but the pain remained. And what would ease that? Not the tears I'd cried or was crying now. Not distance or all the time left in my life. I loved Jonas Luker—loved him, and it seemed I'd turned my world upside down to be the best I could be for him and it hadn't been enough. How I ached to stay in his arms forever, and yet with my heart and soul I wished the trains had been running—wished Jonas were a hundred miles away.

"I love you. Oh, I do love you, honey," Jonas finally said, his mouth brushing my ear. "I don't know why it's been so hard for me to tell you."

It couldn't be true. Hadn't he told me himself he didn't care? But there was that caring look in his eyes I'd seen before.

"I was wrong to get engaged to Melissa. I—I thought I was being wise, but when I tried to explain it to you, I knew it was all wrong. I saw the pain in your eyes, and I hated myself. You shouldn't have run. I wanted to fix it then, and as far as Melissa goes, that night, after Hal had you settled, I rode out and told her. I've certainly spread a lot of grief around. I'm sorry."

"But why did you say you didn't love me, Jonas?"

"I didn't *say* that, honey."

"But Jonas, I remember—"

"Believe me, Lori. You weren't paying much attention by then. I never denied loving you. I just said I was attracted to you and let you take it from there."

It didn't make any sense. "But why—why?"

He released me and stepped away, shaking his head. "Let's go inside and finish this. You're going to be sick and—"

"Jonas, *I want to know now!* If you didn't *say* it, why did you even let me *think* you didn't care?"

"I don't know! I—I—" He threw up his hands and strode back to me. "Just look at you, Lori—"

I glanced down at my mud-caked shoes and my sopping dress and laughed. "Now, you mean?"

"You know what I'm saying—your beauty, your background. I couldn't believe you could love me—not for long. Not when I didn't have the trappings your family would expect your husband to have—the money—"

"But I don't need money." How many times did I have to tell him that?

"Girl"—he touched my cheek—"everybody does. This is mortality, and that's the way it's supposed to be. But I was selling you short. You're a fighter, scrappy and strong-willed, and besides that—I'm desperate to have you." His head went back, his eyes full of challenge. "So what do you say, marry me?"

"Yes, yes. Oh, Jonas!" I reached up and kissed him my answer—kissed and kissed him. After a time he held me away, asking, "When?"

"Whenever you say, darling."

He thrust out his chin then and laughed, a triumphant, ringing, joy-filled sound, and then I was unceremoniously picked up and swung about. The world went flying when Jonas crashed into the wall of the hotel, staggered to regain his balance, and then slipped off the porch altogether. We were both of us down in the mud and the rain, laughing like children.

"You folks all right?"

"Anyone hurt here?"

The door had opened, and several curious strangers strained to see two crazy people lolling about in the mud.

The laughter died on our lips (though not in our hearts), and we were quick to scramble to our feet and sober up. Jonas took my arm firmly and led me around to a water barrel where we cleaned up some before going in, and then, upon entering the hotel, he made arrangements for food, hot baths, and two rooms. Jonas said he wanted one downstairs and one up. We were in love, violently in love, and I suppose he wasn't taking any chances.

TWENTY-FIVE

It was a lovely breakfast tray to be receiving at two in the afternoon. The bacon, eggs, and griddle cakes smelled heavenly, and so did the small bouquet of yellow chrysanthemums that had been set above my plate. For a wild minute I wondered if the flowers might be from Jonas, and then decided it was more likely that the cook, Mabel, had sent them. (Jonas had told her the night before that I'd been unwell, and she'd taken an immediate liking to me and I to her. And she certainly could cook—what a talent that was!)

I ate with relish and then styled my clean hair in a romantically curly topknot and dressed with care in the outfit I'd saved for job-hunting—the slim, stylish tan suit that had never been worn before. I still had a slight headache but otherwise felt terrific. And better than that, I couldn't wait to see my man again. He hadn't come near my room but had been sending up little messages like the one that accompanied this last meal. This time he'd outdone himself. This message had only one misspelled word and absolutely no cross-outs! I smiled, loving Jonas all the more for his outrageous handwriting.

209

> Lori: I here by way of the cook that you're dying to take a walk. If you're up to it, let's go. I'll be waiting downstairs. J

With flowers in hand, I fairly flew down to the dining room, but Jonas wasn't in sight. A large gentleman in a suit stood at the windows, and a group of men deep in conversation sat around one of the tables, stopping at my approach and eyeing me with interest, but Jonas wasn't among them.

"May I help you?" Several shoved back chairs and stood. I had to say something.

"Does anyone have the time?"

"We've got all the time you want!" someone chimed, and his pals snorted with laughter.

I couldn't help but laugh too. It was incredible how everything had turned out so beautifully!

Behind me someone cleared his throat, and I turned to see Jonas, and in a suit! He looked elegant in the extreme. Oh, I'd seen him dressed up for church, but never had he looked so meticulous and fine, and at the moment I was reminded of his gentleman father that he was always so careful not to imitate.

"Was that you at the windows, Jonas?" He took my arm and led me away from the stares of the men to a more private corner near the door.

"Yes, and I see you got my flowers."

So they were from Jonas! I wanted to pinch myself. "Oh, thank you. I love them!"

"You're surprised, aren't you. Probably *dumbfounded*, right?" He tugged at the carefully done tie, pulling it askew.

I readjusted the knot for him and shook my head. "Not at all." I wasn't about to admit anything of the kind. "You're looking very handsome."

"Yeah? Well, let's get out of here." He linked my arm through his and swung open the door.

210   "But where are we going?" I asked as we moved outside.

He nudged the door closed behind us, and then, spying the empty street, he pulled me to him and kissed me hard.

"Courting, Lady. We're going courting." Arm in arm we walked down into the sunshine.